SLEEPING WITH THE FISHES

A Deadline Cozy Mystery Book 6

SONIA PARIN

Copyright © 2017 Sonia Parin
All Rights Reserved

No part of this publication may be reproduced in any form or by any means, without the prior written permission of the author, except in the case of brief quotations embodied in critical articles and reviews

This is a work of fiction. Names, characters, places and incidents are the product of the author's imagination or are used fictitiously. Any resemblance to actual persons, living or dead, organizations, events or locales is entirely coincidental.

ISBN-10: 1545147442

ISBN-13: 978-1545147443

Chapter One

LESS THAN AN HOUR into her forced captivity with fifteen days remaining. She'd never make it, Eve thought as the cool sea breeze swept around her.

A few weeks before she'd been counting down the days and walking on air because she'd finally agreed to take some real time off to relax.

Now...

Eve watched the shoreline disappearing.

Sagging against the railing, she made a point of smiling.

"You'll be pleased to know we arrived safe and sound," she told Jill, her voice light and cheerful.

Jill laughed. "Try saying it with less anxiety in your voice. What's up?"

"It's not anxiety, it's..." Eve sighed and tried to admit to being out of her depth, but her pride stopped her. "Have you ever been to an Elvis convention?" she asked. "Or any convention where everyone is dressed in their elaborate costumes... and you're not."

"Not in this lifetime. Don't tell me there's one on board?"

"Hang on, you're breaking up." Eve leaned over the railing. "Not an Elvis convention. It's a Carmen Miranda glitzy extravaganza. Everywhere I look, there's someone wearing a bunch of bananas on their head. I've boarded the cruise ship from hell."

"Carmen Miranda! But that sounds like fun."

"You'd say that and I thought so too at first, but then I saw their true colors. Ruthless comes to mind. They have this 'get out of my way or be run down' air about them. It's actually scary."

"What I'd give to see you there right now," Jill said in what sounded like teary-eyed laughter.

Eve stared at a woman who was not only dressed to the nines in her Carmen Miranda getup, but was also surrounded by a musical entourage serenading her.

The woman gave Eve a head to toe sweep that felt like fingernails digging into her.

"Eve? Talk to me. I need to know you haven't been pushed overboard."

"Close. One of the impersonators just gave me a death stare."

"Try to play nice," Jill suggested.

"Honestly, I haven't said a word to them."

"You're on a ship... on the water," Jill reasoned,

"Sound travels. Either that or they think you're their competition."

"Why would they think that?"

Jill hummed. "Well... you do have a sort of retro look happening and with the right costume, I'm sure you could give them a run for their money."

Unconvinced, Eve snorted. "As if. I wouldn't be caught dead wearing a pineapple on my head."

"I thought you said it was bananas."

"Let me put it this way, I'd have no trouble throwing together a fruit salad and I wouldn't have to go anywhere near a fruit market."

"Just how many are there?"

"Hard to say. They all look the same, give or take a banana."

"Eve, you're broadcasting your thoughts. They must be picking up on your disapproval."

"Who said I disapprove of them?"

"Your tone?"

Eve harrumphed. "Did I happen to mention one of them already shoved me... quite unceremoniously, out of her way?"

"No, you didn't."

"Well, she also threw in a few expletives."

"You must have said something to aggravate her."

"I might have suggested she tone it down a bit. There are kids around. Hang on. I'm taking a photo of this. You need to see it." Just as she snapped a photo, the Carmen Miranda impersonator who had earlier on given her a scathing look stuck her elbow out and jabbed another Carmen Miranda in the ribs. "Oh..."

"What?"

"There's a Carmen Miranda rumble about to erupt." Another woman burst in on the scene. Eve stood well out of hearing range but going by the hand gestures, she'd guess they were exchanging more than a few harsh words. "Okay, it's on its way. I only wish I could send myself off."

"Don't be so melodramatic, Eve. What's the worst that can happen?"

"Apart from losing my cell signal... I don't know." She rolled her eyes. "I could be marooned on an island with them."

Jill said something but the signal dropped off.

"Jill. Are you there?" she asked, her tone desperate.

"You might be right," Jill's voice crackled slightly. "This cruise might not have been the best idea for you. Is it too early for a drink?"

"I think they saw me coming. Waiters have been plying me with tropical drinks since I arrived. I thought it would help settle me down, but now I'm thinking I need my wits about me. I can't let Mira see me like this. As far as she knows, I'm here to have the best time of my life. That means I need to dump all my angst on you. Sorry." Although Eve doubted her aunt would notice. She'd fallen behind on her next book and was facing another deadline so would most likely be too busy to even come up for breath.

"You're suffering from first day jitters. Relax. Enjoy. Remember, you've got an inn to set up. It'll probably be ages before you can take another vacation."

"That's just it. What was I thinking taking time off now? I'm about to open a business I don't know the first thing about. People will be depending on me to provide a service... to employ them..."

"Think of the positives. What's your cabin like?"

Eve drew in a shaky breath. "It's simple, which is a lovely respite from the rest of the ship. Think of Vegas and you'll get the idea. Lots of gold trim clashing with pastel colors. Remind me to steer clear of them for the inn. No peach, lilac, cream or beige..."

"Positives, Eve. You're straying."

"Okay. The bed felt comfortable when I collapsed on it. Then again, a wooden plank would have been heaven after all the waiting around I did." Eve listened to the silence. "Did you just roll your eyes?"

"Do you blame me?"

No. She didn't. She'd only ever gone on working vacations. She should be over the moon happy. Instead... "Boarding a cruise ship is hard work," Eve complained. "The security checkpoints got me a bit rattled. I'm sure I look like a maniac on the photo, which I had no idea they were going to take. If anything happens on this ship, I'm going to be the prime suspect." She raked her fingers through her hair. "I'm not cut out for this."

"A life of leisure?" Jill laughed.

"It's not that. I can relax. I'm sure I can. I know I

can. It's just... all the fake tans and over the top chirpiness, not to mention the toothpaste commercial bleached smiles... it's all too much. I'm all for happiness, but this is too contrived."

"Careful, it might be contagious."

"Don't joke. After we checked in, Mira took me to the top deck. That's when the drinking started. Everyone was super happy and pumped with excitement and waving at imaginary people on the dock. I caught the bug and I swear I had tears in my eyes when the ship slipped away from the pier. Now that I think about it, the Carmen Miranda scuffle is a breath of fresh air." Eve shook her head. "Okay, I just heard myself."

"Actually, you might be right. A cruise was a huge step for you. Maybe you should have started with a weekend away. Chip away the workaholic in you a tiny layer at a time."

"Jill, I've already had a few months on the island to wind down—"

"Your time on the island doesn't count. Think about all the killers who've come after you."

Several more Carmen Miranda lookalikes had joined in the argument. Fingers were pointed. Expletives exchanged. Before anyone could draw blood, a man stepped in and somehow managed to pacify everyone. He didn't appear to favor anyone in particular, but Eve noticed all the women responded to his call for calm without any arguments.

"Killjoy," Eve said under her breath.

"What? Did someone get killed?" Jill asked.

"No, but I almost wish someone had. I think I've become addicted to murder and mayhem. Why didn't you talk me out of this? You must have known I'd go stir crazy."

"Think of me, I'm surrounded by your paint and fabric swatches. Oh, and boxes. Too many to count. Linen. Cutlery. Pots. Pans."

"Sorry, on our way to New York I insisted we stop by a catering supplier and I went a bit overboard. By the way, thank you for staying at the inn."

"Are you grateful enough to offer me permanent residency? I need to get out of my parents' place. They're driving me batty with their squabbling. Dad's got his eye on a new Winnebago and mom's set her heart on a trip to Hawaii. I'm in the middle and I'm afraid that even after they sort this argument out, they'll find something else to bicker about. If I don't get out now... well, I might do something."

"A room at the inn? If that's what you want, go for it. Or maybe we could convert the space above the stables for you."

"Hang on. It sounds as if I missed my chance to ask for more."

"This is interesting," Eve said changing the subject.

"What?"

"That man who broke up the scuffle. He's walking away now and all the impersonators are following him."

"And?"

"They all have goofy, adoring smiles on their faces. If they all have their eyes on him, we could be in for more than just a bit of elbowing."

"See, I knew you'd cheer up. You only needed a hint of trouble."

Eve groaned. "I can't be that person. I'm... too run of the mill normal."

"Aha. That's why you're freaked out by the impersonators."

"Well... think about it. People pretending to be what they're not. There's a lot of scope there. Who knows what they're hiding behind those fake personas?" Eve drew in a big breath. "Yoga. I saw it on one of the brochures. Yes... that's what I'll do. Spend my trip mastering the art of relaxation. Thanks for being my sounding board, Jill. Talk to you soon."

Eve returned to her cabin, along the way making sure she steered clear of anyone wearing a costume. However, her efforts were futile. They'd taken over the ship. Thoughts of being decked by a pineapple had her hurrying her steps.

Inside her cabin, she leaned against the door and sighed with relief.

Her aunt Mira looked up from her laptop. "Glad to see you haven't jumped ship."

"Am I that obvious?" She collapsed on the bed and stared at a painting of a woman dressed in 1920s clothing. In those days, casual meant wearing suits and hats, with gloves not far behind. Kicking off her sandals, Eve smiled as she thought of the five new pair of shorts she'd packed for the trip.

Mira chuckled. "I'm surprised you're not hyperventilating."

"Sorry. I don't know what's come over me."

Mira hummed under her breath. "I expected to see a hint of cabin fever, but it hasn't even been a day. Maybe you've had too much excitement in your life lately and you're finding all this too sedate."

"Hardly." Eve chortled. "You wouldn't say that if you'd seen the Carmen Miranda brawl."

Mira smiled. "Trust you to come across a bit of excitement. I saw them mentioned on the program. It's their tenth anniversary cruise. They're going to commemorate it with a competition for best Carmen Miranda impersonator."

A competition. That would definitely raise the stakes. Eve bit the edge of her lip. This was one spectacle she needed to stay away from. "I've decided to look into the yoga classes on board. I think it'll do me a world of good. Force me to focus on relaxing."

"That's jumping in at the deep end. You should work up to it. Get a massage first," Mira suggested.

Eve sat up and dug her fingers into her shoulder. "You know me too well."

"You've had too many close encounters with killers, Eve. I think you're suffering from fight or flight syndrome. You need to shake it off."

Eve gave a pensive nod. Mira had a point. Maybe

she should look into a meditation class. She swung her legs off the couch and sat up. "How's your book coming along?"

Mira stretched her arms over her head. "My hero thinks he knows what's best for the heroine and that's landed him in a heap of trouble."

"What about the mad innkeeper? How's she doing?"

"Turns out she's been working undercover. I've turned her into a spy. She's investigating the hero."

"Is this where the heroine steps in and saves the day?"

Mira's mouth gaped open. "You've been reading my manuscript."

"I snuck a peak." Only after she'd discovered her aunt had fashioned the innkeeper after her. "Please tell me you're not going to kill the innkeeper."

"Kill her? Oh, no. I've been plotting an outline for her. She's getting her own story. That's why I've fallen behind with this book."

Eve clapped her hands. "You're turning me into a heroine?"

Mira laughed. "You still think I modeled my mad innkeeper on you?"

Eve gave her aunt a raised eyebrow look.

"Okay, there might be some similarities..."

Hearing a knock at the door, Eve went to answer it. Seeing it was the porter with their luggage, she dug inside her pocket and drew out a bill for the tip. "Our luggage is here." She wheeled their suitcases in and put hers on the bed.

"Now you have no excuse, you'll have to take up yoga. Unless you didn't bring any yoga pants with you."

"Actually... now that I think about it, I didn't. I guess I'll have to hit the shops."

"Oh, they're going to love you. These ships are a shopaholic's paradise."

"Wait a minute. This isn't my luggage." Eve held up a white top that would barely cover her. "Check yours."

Mira unlocked her suitcase and after a brief look said, "Yes, all here."

Frowning, Eve went through the rest of the clothes and pulled out a plastic fruit salad headdress. "It's a Carmen Miranda smorgasbord."

Mira threw her head back and laughed. "Marvelous. You can join in the fun now."

"The porter must be dyslexic. He inverted the last two numbers on the tag. I better hurry and catch up with him." By the time she rolled the suitcase out, the porter had disappeared. Eve crossed her fingers and hoped the other person had her suitcase. As she strode along the hallway checking the cabin numbers she saw a woman emerge from one of the cabins, her head covered with a turban embellished with fruit.

When Eve reached the cabin, she realized it was the one she'd been looking for.

She called out to the woman, but either she didn't hear her or she'd decided to ignore her.

Eve rushed after her, but before she could reach her, the woman disappeared inside the elevator.

Okay.

She had to return the suitcase and get hers back.

On the off chance there might be someone else in the cabin, Eve knocked on the door.

It eased open. Not because someone had opened it, but because it hadn't been locked properly.

"Hello," she called out. "I think I have your suitcase and I'm hoping you have mine."

No one answered. Eve checked the corridor. Just her luck. No staff at hand to help her.

"Hello," she called out again. "I'm coming in." At this point, Eve knew she should be wondering why no one had answered. Without giving it much thought she decided the woman she'd seen rush off hadn't closed the door properly.

She considered her options but decided against chasing after her. Surely no one would mind if she retrieved her suitcase. In fact, she'd be doing everyone a favor since she'd also make sure she locked the door behind her.

Taking a tentative step, she peered inside the cabin. At first glance everything appeared to be normal, then Eve noticed the fruit on the floor. Cherries. Bananas. A pineapple. She followed the trail and gazed out the floor to ceiling sliding door. It stood open.

"Okay. This does not look good but I don't want to jump to conclusions because if I do, Jill will accuse me of being a death knell." With her gaze fixed on a colorful scarf hanging on the railing, she released her hold on the suitcase and urged her feet to move toward the balcony. "For all I know, a light breeze swept it out there." Yet when she reached the railing her first impulse was to look overboard.

And just as well she did...

Chapter Two
___

EVE COUNTED to three and then entered the cabin she shared with Mira.

She'd made up her mind to enjoy the trip and, despite her reservations, she was willing to use anything and everything in her arsenal of personal inducements to make sure she made the best of this cruise and didn't ruin it for Mira.

Her aunt remained the one person Eve didn't ever want to disappoint. In Mira, Eve found acceptance. She could be the person she wanted to be without having to apologize for it. This was something she didn't get from her parents who'd never come to terms with her decision to go into the food industry instead of following in their footsteps. At least she didn't have to suffer their disapproval... Their high-flying careers as lawyers meant she only got to see them once a year for Christmas, if they could spare the time.

"I see you've found your suitcase."

"Yes, all's good." Somehow, Eve managed to keep her tone normal.

Setting her suitcase down on the edge of the bed, she opened it and began unpacking.

Days before she'd been kidding around with Jack, trying to make light of the reasons for coming on the cruise. After her close encounter with a killer she'd decided to take Mira up on her suggestion to accompany her on the cruise. The spur of the moment decision had surprised her. Eve had been working in the restaurant business from a young age and had never taken vacations, but Mira had talked her into it, suggesting she needed a new experience.

Jack, what should I take on my vacation?
Leave the gun take the cannoli...

That had been Jack's way of telling her to stay out of trouble. Detective Jack Bradford knew her only too well.

Eve's shoulders slumped. "What was I thinking bringing this swimsuit? I bought it a couple of years ago and never wore it." She held it against her and tried to imagine squeezing into it.

"Um, Eve?"

"Yes?" Eve turned and faced Mira, her expression, she hoped, neutral. Not that it mattered as Mira hadn't looked up from her computer.

"Mind telling me what happened?"

"I probably put on weight. It's really strange because the scales tell me I still weigh the same. In fact, the only time my weight varies is when I work on new cake recipes. It got really bad when I was trying to improve my chocolate cake recipe. Jill's partly to blame for that. She kept saying there was something missing. Anyhow... the weight piled on. It usually takes me a couple of months to shake off the excess—"

"I wasn't referring to your swimsuit not fitting." Mira's tone remained conversational.

"Oh?"

"For a moment there I thought those couple of drinks I had when we boarded had come back to haunt me." Mira sighed. "And, as immersed as I am in my story, I still noticed the ship slowing down."

"I don't know what you're talking about."

Mira glanced up. "If you don't, then why are you so pale?"

Eve pinched her cheeks. "The elevators are fast. I think I left my stomach on the lower deck."

"Was that before or after the ship came to a full stop?"

Right after the captain had questioned her, actually. Eve huffed out a breath. "I was hoping you hadn't noticed that."

Mira's eyebrows rose into a neat curve.

"Okay. It was a long shot." She rummaged through her suitcase. No yoga pants.

She didn't have a chance in hell of relaxing now.

"Eve."

"All right. You're going to find out anyway so I might as well tell you. There's been... an incident on board."

"An incident?" Mira held her gaze.

Eve decided it really was better out than in. "There's been a murder on board."

Mira gave a small nod. "Care to repeat that and add all the details you're obviously leaving out?" She closed her laptop and strode over to the mini bar to pour herself a drink. "Come out to the balcony. We'll talk there."

"Um... the balcony. Right... well... If it's okay with you, I'd rather stand here."

"Eve."

She hung her head and followed her aunt. "Please don't tell anyone what I just told you. The captain assures me it was an accident."

"And you don't think it is."

She told Mira about her efforts to return the suitcase. "When I saw the scarf on the railing my first instinct was to search the water and sure enough, I could still see the woman floating. Hard to miss her in her colorful outfit," she said, her tone conversational even as her heart pounded against her chest. "I called for help. The captain notified the coast guard and he organized a rescue boat. That's when the ship slowed down... The coast guard was nearby so they got to her first and retrieved the body."

"Do we know who it is?"

Eve slumped down on a chair and gazed out to sea. "There's a head count underway to make sure they have the right person, but we can safely assume it was the occupant of cabin 4021. One of the Carmen Miranda impersonators."

Mira studied her for long seconds. "What makes you think she was killed?"

The odds were stacked in favor of it.

"Please tell me you're not thinking you had anything to do with it."

"Well..."

"Eve."

"What are the chances of this being a coincidence? Within hours of me coming on board a cruise ship someone is killed," she blurted out.

"That's nonsense and you know it."

"The victim had my suitcase," Eve insisted.

"That happens."

"I've been grumbling about the Carmen Miranda impersonators on board and, surprise, surprise, the victim is one of them."

"Nothing but coincidence, Eve."

Eve ran through the conversation she'd had with Jill. Had she mentioned death, or killing? "I might have set the ball rolling. You know, what you think about, you bring about."

"As my heroine would say, that's balderdash," Mira insisted.

"So you think it's normal for a passenger to fall overboard?"

"I'm not an expert on the subject, but it's been known to happen."

"Right. It was just happenstance that our luggage got mixed up and that I happened to go knocking on the victim's door moments before she jumped... or was pushed off the ship. And what are the odds of her also being one of the Carmen Miranda impersonators?" She surged to her feet. "It's official. I'm cursed."

The tone of her cell phone ringing snapped her out of her pity party. Panic took hold of her. "It's Jack. What do I do? What do I say?"

"You could try saying hello," Mira suggested.

"And the moment I do, he'll know something's happened."

"When did you become so uptight?"

"Right after the first murder on the island and I've been doing my best to hide it." She drew in a quivering breath and giving a small nod, answered. "Jack. Hi. Hello. Howdy-ho. How wonderful to hear from you."

Mira rolled her eyes. "Too obvious," she mouthed.

"Eve."

Jack had used the 'pass the salt, please' tone. She was sure he had... "Yes?"

"Please tell me you had nothing to do with this murder," Jack said.

Murder!

"I knew it. She was killed." Eve frowned. "How...

how did you know? How did you find out about it? Hang on. I'm putting you on speaker..."

"Coast guard. One of the rookies at the station was on the phone talking to a friend who works there. So... did you have anything to do with it?"

This time, she picked up a hint of wariness in his voice. Perhaps even concern. "That depends on how you define my involvement."

"Did you know the victim?"

"Really, Jack? How could I? I only boarded the ship this morning." And shortly after arriving on the island... a body had turned up. She really didn't have a good track record. "Are you, by any chance, interrogating me?" Eve asked.

"It's out of my jurisdiction, but... I have a vested interest."

"Because you think I'm involved." Her voice hitched, "Where's your trust?"

Jack chuckled. "I trust you. I just don't trust a killer on the loose. Now try to calm down."

"I am serenity personified." She had no trouble picturing the edge of his eyes crinkling with amusement.

"Good. So are you going to tell me what happened?"

"Detective, you assume too much. What makes you think I am in any way involved?" She heard Mira chuckle. "Actually, don't answer that. I don't want our relationship ruined. And it might do me good to run through the sequence of events. I might have missed something." She closed her eyes and pictured everything from the moment she stepped out of her cabin. Halfway through telling Jack what had happened, she stopped. "Are you taking notes?"

"I might be."

"A moment ago you said you trusted me."

"From what I understand, you were the first on the scene. Tell me again exactly what you saw."

"Shouldn't the police come on board?"

"You've already reached international waters. The police will no doubt want to talk to you when you dock in Florida."

She ran everything through her mind again. "I'm thinking there might have been a fight. A scuffle. Some sort of struggle. I saw clothing strewn on the floor and a headdress. Some of the fruit had come off."

"Fruit?"

"The victim was part of the Carmen Miranda convention." Eve tapped her chin. "I wonder if the victim was on the upper deck?"

"Why? Did something happen?"

"There was an altercation earlier on. I was on the phone with Jill. Everyone was dressed in their costumes. Hard to tell them apart. Except..."

"What?"

"I had no trouble spotting the body floating because the colors were so garish. Bright lime green and fluorescent orange."

"So while everyone is dressed as Carmen Miranda, they're all wearing different costumes?"

"Yes. They're quite unique."

"She was a colorful performer," Mira piped in.

"Hang on." She tried to bring up the image of the altercation in her mind. There had been five... maybe six women involved and they'd each worn a different outfit. "I need some coloring pencils."

Mira strode back inside the cabin and returned shortly with her laptop. Eve watched as she opened one of the applications and used one of the tools to draw a figure.

"That's quite good, Mira. I didn't know you could draw."

"I sometimes do this to sketch out scenes for my books. How many did you say there were?"

"Five... maybe six."

Mira put the finishing touches to the first figure then she copied and pasted six more figures. "What color do you remember them wearing?"

"The first one wore orange and turquoise. And she had a white turban on with a pineapple."

"And the woman you saw floating wore lime green and fluorescent orange."

"Yes."

"Do you remember seeing her on deck?" Jack asked.

"I'll have to think about it. Let's do the others. There was the purple one. She had a yellow turban with bright red cherries." Eve clicked her fingers. "And then there was the silver one. Her turban had a pineapple on it with bananas. She's the one who gave me the death stare."

Jack groaned. "So you did have contact with them."

"Not deliberately. I was up on deck talking with Jill and fast losing my cell connection. My phone's now switched over to the on board satellite and that's going to cost an arm and a leg. Anyway, I was focused on the conversation with Jill. Wait..." Eve held up a finger. "One of them shoved me out of the way."

This time Jack sighed. "You got into a fight with a passenger?"

"No. I was making my way from one end of the ship to the other. Then... there was the death stare. That happened when I was walking toward the railing. I told you my cell signal was failing. The further we moved away from land... Never mind all that. The one who shoved me probably thought I was moving too slowly or I wasn't moving to the rhythm. Did I mention the music? One of them had her own entourage and she was making a grand entrance."

"Music?"

"Yes and singing. You know... Chica chica bom chic."

"Okay. What else do you remember?"

"The silver Miranda elbowed the purple one in the ribs. Then the—"

"Wait. Who shoved you out of the way?"

"That's a good question. I know the silver Miranda gave me the death stare and she then elbowed the purple Miranda. Let me think... I saw a flash of green and..."

"Orange?" Mira asked.

"Yes."

"Then you were shoved by the murder victim. You said she wore lime green and fluorescent orange."

"That's right. And she's the one who jumped in and argued with the silver Miranda."

"Did you hear any of it?"

"No. It looked like a territorial war. Lime green and fluorescent orange kept pointing to the other end of the ship. I guess the police can get to the bottom of it all. I've decided I'm staying in my cabin for the duration of the cruise."

Mira cleared her throat. "You haven't finished describing the costumes."

Eve did a quick mental check. "Oh, did I mention the one with the sailor outfit? She didn't have any fruit on her, but she wore the most garish necklaces. Bright purple, orange and green. Her turban had a sailor's hat attached to it."

"That's four counting the victim."

"Hang on, there's one more. She wore fire engine red and blue and had a red turban with bananas on it. Did you get all that, Jack?"

"I'm almost afraid to say yes."

Mira clapped her hands. "You've color coded all the suspects."

"Wait. Are we pointing the finger of suspicion at them?" Eve asked.

Mira shrugged. "Of course. They'd been arguing. It stands to reason there was a lot of competitive animosity between them. It would only take one person to go one step too far."

Jack cleared his throat. "Eve, go back to when you returned the suitcase. Did you see anyone else?"

"Yes. Yes, I did."

Mira shifted to the edge of her chair. Eve couldn't help thinking her aunt had been showing more interest in the incident than she normally would. A sign she had writer's block?

"I saw someone coming out of cabin 4021."

"By someone, do you mean—"

"Yes, a Carmen Miranda impersonator." Forgetting herself, she stood up and leaned against the railing. "Give me a minute. I have all these colors whizzing around my mind. I remember white, lots of it..." Or silver... "And a colorful sash around her waist. I can't be sure if I saw her out on the deck."

"But you're sure you saw her emerge from cabin 4021."

"Yes. Positive. I called out to her but she either didn't hear me or she ignored me. Also, at that point I wasn't sure I had the right cabin. By the time I checked, she'd already disappeared inside the elevator."

"Did she look disheveled?"

"No. Are you wondering if she'd been in a fight with the victim?"

"I'm trying to catch anything you might have missed."

Eve raked her fingers through her hair. "Now that I

think about it, she might have been adjusting her turban, but that doesn't really mean anything." Eve sighed. "There's a hoard of Carmen Miranda impersonators running around and they're all fussing with their costumes."

"But at that precise moment when you approached cabin 4021, you only saw one. Correct?"

"Yes, detective."

Mira held up her hand. "I did a Google search on procedures aboard cruise ships. Do we know if they're up to date with cameras? Most ships nowadays have warning systems in place to raise the alarm if someone falls overboard. The camera might have captured something."

"Are you suggesting I approach the captain and ask him?" Eve shook her head. "He's not too happy with me."

"Why?"

"Because I had the gumption to walk into someone else's cabin. He couldn't see past that. Never mind that I raised the alarm."

"Maybe the captain is in on it," Mira suggested.

"You're kidding me."

"It's something I picked up from you Eve. Suspect everyone acting suspiciously. Why would the captain be cross with you? If you hadn't raised the alarm, the ship would have continued on its way and the woman's body would have been lost for good."

"You're right. Now all we need is motive. Any ideas, Jack?"

"I'm afraid to open my mouth in case it gives you ideas and you think you can go off and launch an investigation."

Eve shook her head. "That's not going to happen. I've already decided, I'm staying right here in this cabin and living off room service until we hit dry land." To make her point clear, she folded her arms and pursed her lips.

Mira gazed at her. "That's no way to spend you cruise."

True. She'd come here to relax but if she set foot outside the cabin, she'd be looking over her shoulder and wondering if every person she encountered had murder on their mind. "I'll read." She shrugged. "You spend most of your time in the cabin writing."

"I do write, but I also go out to dinner and watch movies. They have the Starlight Cinema on this cruise. It's quite lovely to sit out there, a glass of champagne in hand, the sea breeze wafting around..."

Perfect place to make oneself a sitting target... "I can gaze out to sea. I'm told it's very therapeutic." Eve lifted her chin. Then... she lowered it a notch at a time. Her lips parted. "I've just remembered something."

Mira sighed and slumped back on her chair.

She, more than anyone else, knew what came next...

"I took a photo of the Carmen Miranda scuffle."

Chapter Three

"WHAT'S TAKING JACK SO LONG?" Eve wrung her hands. She swirled around, strode back inside the cabin and within seconds came out to the balcony again. "I sent him that photo hours ago. Jack wouldn't leave me out of the loop now. He wouldn't."

Mira chuckled but didn't look up from the book she'd been reading. "So much for not getting involved."

Eve gave a brisk shake of her head. "At the risk of sounding paranoid, what if the Carmen Miranda I saw walking out of the cabin finds out I saw her. She could jump to conclusions and think I can actually identify her. I'll become a target." That type of thinking, she knew, resulted from too many close calls with killers.

"We should make sure the cabin is secure. Check to see if the door is properly locked," Mira suggested.

"You're making fun of me."

"On the contrary, I'm taking you seriously. And I'm

now thinking if the killer is determined, he or she might coerce the busboy into slipping something in your food."

"Where's this coming from, Mira? You don't usually try to rattle my nerves."

Mira sat back and steepled her fingers under her chin. "I'm not sure. Maybe it's about me turning my innkeeper into a spy. I'm developing a devious mind."

"I wish you wouldn't. One disturbed person in the family is surely enough." Eve pressed her hand against her stomach.

"That's a serious hunger rumble, loud enough for me to hear."

Eve cringed. "I missed lunch."

"Why don't you change clothes and we'll go to dinner. I made reservations for us."

"When?"

"While we were still at home. You have to think ahead on cruises. Everything fills up quickly."

Had the murder victim thought ahead? Of course she had. She'd probably obsessed about her costume and the entire Carmen Miranda anniversary get-together. All that planning hadn't done her any good. "I'm not sure about mingling with a possible killer."

"I'll be with you the whole time."

She strolled around the cabin again and came to a stop. "I can't believe the captain didn't take me seriously. People don't just fall off balconies." It scared her to think something so dreadful could happen with no positive action taken by the authorities. If not for Jack, the matter would not be investigated until it was too late.

"They do fall off if they've been drinking too much or if they're clumsy. I've seen some of those impersonators and they were all wearing killer heels."

Eve looked out the window toward the balcony. "No. It doesn't make any sense. The railing is high enough to prevent anyone from falling accidentally." She lifted her chin. "Someone pushed her."

"Here's another possibility," Mira offered. "As unpalatable as it might sound, she might have been suicidal."

Eve swung toward Mira. "You must really be stuck with your book. You never come up with so many theories."

"And you usually have Jill to play around with ideas. I'm trying to compensate for her absence. Now go get dressed. I can hear my stomach beginning to grumble."

"Thanks for humoring me." Eve went through her clothes and selected a simple black dress to wear.

Could one of the Carmen Miranda impersonators be responsible? And if so, why? What would compel someone to commit murder at sea? Did it have something to do with the competition? "How competitive does someone have to be to commit murder?"

"Passionately so," Mira exclaimed.

"I think if we dig around we might find a motive

that sticks because I'm not buying it. No one can possibly be that fiercely competitive. There has to be another reason for murder." She picked up the brochure and scanned through it. "There isn't even a money prize. It's all about the glory of being the best impersonator."

"To some, that could mean a great deal," Mira reasoned. "Think about it. All year round you lead a dull life and this is your one chance to shine. You'd do anything to come out on top."

"What? And then celebrate my moment of glory in prison?" Eve shook her head. "No. Nothing would be worth it." She rolled her shoulders. Not that it did any good. Her neck muscles still felt stiff. "I'm going to book a massage."

"I'll do that for you. Go shower and change. We're going to dinner even if I have to drag you kicking and screaming. Nothing is going to happen to you in the middle of a public restaurant."

"You obviously haven't read enough thrillers or watched crime shows on TV. I could be poisoned right in the middle of the restaurant. The killer could be plotting my demise as we speak."

"You're looking glamorous." Mira wore a jacket and skirt ensemble in vintage pink satin with an elegant strand of pearls around her neck and matching earrings.

"So is everyone else. Look around you."

"It feels like opening night at the opera." The men wore tuxedos while the women accompanying them shone in their stylish gowns and glittering jewels and perfectly applied make-up with not a hair out of place. "You never said this would be a glitzy affair."

"I assumed you knew. Sorry. But would it have made any difference?"

"No." She owned a few dresses. All simple cuts. The style that never went out of fashion. And all black. "I'd never be able to justify buying something to wear only once."

"You would if you went out more often."

"I suppose I can always accessorize to make it go the distance." Yet she'd still be lost in a sea of glamour.

Eve looked around her and took in the extravagant decorations. Every surface appeared to sparkle. A massive chandelier hung in the centre of the restaurant; the flickering lights making it look like a cascade. Lavish flower arrangements were scattered right throughout the restaurant with smaller bouquets on each table, all white flowers. Primroses, lilies, and tulips and a few others she couldn't identify, highlighted with splashes of lime green foliage, and, Eve noticed on closer inspection, slices of lime.

They were shown to a table by the window. Not that Eve could appreciate the ocean view. Her eyes skipped from table to table, committing faces to memory, watching gestures, watching people's reaction to her presence. If anyone threw daggers her way, she wanted to be able to see them. She spotted a table full of Carmen Miranda impersonators but didn't recognize any of the ones she'd seen on deck earlier that day.

"Those must be the non-competitive ones," Eve murmured, and noticed they all chatted together amicably.

"And yet they're all dressed up in their costumes. That's taking their passion seriously," Mira remarked.

"Okay, I caught a furtive glance thrown our way."

Mira cleared her throat. "You mean, your way."

Eve took a sip of water. "Disowning me, Mira?"

"If word got out that you're the one who alerted the captain, then you're the one who'll be a person of interest to the killer. Not me."

"What if the killer wants to get to me through you?"

"Now who is being sinister?"

"Gee. I hope I didn't spoil your dinner."

Mira's attention shifted. "There's more of them coming in."

Eve took a discreet peek. "Oh, yes. They're the ones I saw on deck. Why would they be sitting together? I'd swear they were archenemies."

"Maybe they're bonding in a time of crisis. Or maybe they're all in it together."

That hadn't crossed her mind. "Is there a name for a group of killers?"

"A gang? It doesn't sound right, but I'm sure that's it. Maybe no one has thought of coming up with a name because killers tend to work alone." Mira tilted her head as if in deep thought. "A group of killer whales is called a pod. That's an interesting one..."

Eve's eyes widened. Another group came into the restaurant. "Just how many are there."

"A hundred."

"What?"

"Well, ninety nine now that one of them has been murdered."

Eve focused her attention on the group she recognized. "They're talking to each other but I'm guessing they're putting on an act for the sake of appearances."

A wave of murmured conversations mingled with the tinkling of a piano tune, the sort of music that served as a backdrop and didn't resonate with any real emotions.

Eve pressed the tips of her fingers against her wrist. She might feel comatose but her heart still beat strong.

Catching her action, Mira smiled. "The waiter is coming our way. Have you decided what you're going to have?"

"No. You order for me, please," Eve said as her cell phone rang. Before it could ring again, Eve snatched it off the table and answered it. "Jack. Any news?"

"Yes, my colleagues managed to convince the captain to secure the cabin until they can board the ship."

"They want to dust for prints?" Eve asked.

"We want to preserve the crime scene so the police

can look at the scene with their own eyes when they board."

Eve looked around her and lowered her voice. "What assurance do you have it hasn't already been disturbed?"

"None. We'll have to work with what we have. How are things up your end? Have you learned anything new?"

"Jack, are you encouraging me to question the passengers?"

"It would help if you keep your eyes open for any suspicious behavior. You can learn a lot from a safe distance. I'm not telling you to go out of your way to snoop."

"Of course not. You'd never do that." She took a sip of the wine Mira had ordered and smiled in appreciation. "What about the photo I sent you? Did you come up with anything?"

"We cross-referenced your photos with the passenger I.D. photos. Getting those was no easy task. None of the passengers came up in our database."

"So they don't have a criminal record. That doesn't mean anything. They could be first timers. This could be the first in a killing spree. There were one hundred Carmen Miranda impersonators. Imagine if someone has set out to rid the world of them. I guess we'll have to wait and see." She groaned. "I can't believe I said that."

"This will cheer you up. The photo helped with

narrowing down the time of death. You took it at eleven in the morning. The victim is actually in the picture."

Eve frowned. Strange. She didn't recall seeing anyone wearing those colors until she'd seen the woman floating in the water. Yet when she'd talked it through with Mira and Jack, her mind had caught a flash of lime green and orange. Was her mind playing tricks with her?

"Did you say eleven?"

"Yes."

And she'd gone to the victim's cabin at midday. That meant the lime green and fluorescent orange Carmen Miranda had been killed between eleven and midday... "That's a start." A sixty-minute window of opportunity for one person to do the evil deed. Could they narrow that time frame down?

While Mira burned the midnight oil trying to finish a chapter, Eve tried to remember everything she'd seen in the cabin. Had she touched anything? She wouldn't want the police to find her fingerprints. From experience, she knew that would put her in a tenuous position and at the receiving end of some difficult questions.

She turned to her side and stared blankly into space. If her suitcase hadn't been mixed up, she would never have reported the incident. It might have been at least a day before anyone noticed the woman missing. Maybe even longer. Housekeeping wouldn't necessarily become suspicious if they didn't find any wet towels or an untidy room. They'd probably be grateful.

"Most cases of people perishing at sea are found to be accidental," Mira said.

Eve blinked but didn't answer.

"Don't pretend to be asleep. You've been tossing and turning for the past hour."

"Are you researching?"

"Yes. Interestingly, there are over a hundred deaths at sea each year. A realistic number considering the number of elderly people traveling at any given time. While those deaths aren't suspicious, there are some that raise questions."

Eve plumped up her pillow. "They were too obvious."

"Who?"

"At dinner. The Carmen Miranda group. When I first saw them, they were at each other's throats. Then suddenly, they were on their best behavior."

"One of their own died. Like I said, maybe the death brought them together. You know, bygones."

"I'm not convinced."

"You think they're covering for each other? That wouldn't make sense. If their dislike of each other is so intense, they'd want to start pointing fingers," Mira reasoned.

Eve closed her eyes. At dinner, she'd noticed one of the women had stood up to make a toast. Something in the way she'd lifted her hand to her turban had caught her attention. Eve groaned.

"What?"

"The woman I'm sure came out of the cabin as I was approaching it. I only saw her back, but I know it was the silver Carmen Miranda." The one who'd given her the death stare. The one who'd stood up to make a toast. "She's at the centre of all this."

Eve emerged from the bathroom dressed in her shorts and t-shirt and padded across the room to find the sandals she'd kicked off the day before.

A brand new day, she thought. Time to start enjoying her cruise. Turning to admire the clear blue sky, she noticed Mira had her cell phone pressed to her ear. Eve barely had time to enjoy the clear sky and calm waters.

"Here she is." Mira handed the phone to Eve. "It's Jack. He rang a couple of times while you were in the shower so I thought I'd put him out of his misery."

"Thanks." She grabbed a bottle of water and strode out to the balcony. "Ahoy there. What news?"

"You sound chirpy this morning."

Eve smiled. Then she remembered her last waking thought. Would she be able to pick the woman who'd come out of the cabin from a line-up simply by looking at her hand gesture? How certain could she be it had been the silver Miranda? "Sorry to say it's already faded. Please tell me you have something concrete to go on with."

"There's a retired detective on board. I've been in contact with him and told him to keep an eye out for you. David Bergstrom's been brought in as a consultant to ensure the crime scene remains sealed."

"Good to hear you refer to it as a crime scene."

Jack cleared his throat and that usually meant he had information he didn't necessarily wish to share with her. Before she could prod, he surprised her.

"We have no choice. The autopsy report came in."

"I get the feeling I should sit down."

"There's evidence of blunt force trauma." He gave her a moment for the information to sink in. "Eve, do you remember seeing anything in the cabin that might have been used as a weapon?"

"No. Then again, I didn't search for a weapon. My priority was to raise the alarm."

"David Bergstrom will gain access to the cabin today. Perhaps you could go in with him and check to see if anything has been disturbed."

Another pause. This time Eve heard a hint of hesitation.

"Eve."

"Yes?" she asked coyly.

"Don't take this as leeway to go rogue on me. David's in charge. He sets the boundaries and you're going to stick to them. Do you hear me?"

"Aye aye captain."

David Bergstrom's striking good looks had Mira lost for words. Eve's gaze bounced between her aunt's dazzled expression and David's equally interested gaze.

He looked to be about fifty something. If he was any older, he did well to hide it. His strong physique spoke of regular physical activity. Broad shoulders, flat stomach. The few lines on his face were mostly laugh lines, which boded well for Mira. She liked a man with a healthy sense of humor.

"Jack mentioned you'd be dropping by to introduce yourself."

It took a moment for David Bergstrom to tear his attention away from Mira. They'd been having breakfast and trying to focus on the delectable fare when he'd approached their table.

"Care to join us?" Eve asked.

"I'd love to."

"This is my aunt Mira. She's an author."

"Mira Lloyd? The name rings a bell. Actually, I'm thinking of Elizabeth Lloyd."

"That's her."

He gazed at Mira, his eyes unblinking. Finally, he gave her a small smile. "My wife was a fan of your historical romances. I have to admit to having read a few of them myself... okay, I've read as many as you've published. It made for interesting conversation over breakfast after a late night reading session. We used to compare notes."

A delicate shade of pink bloomed on Mira's cheeks. Eve had never seen her in such a state of awe.

"Sadly she died a couple of years ago."

As they commiserated with him, Eve wondered if the cruise was his way of getting on with his life.

"Where do you live when you're not on a cruise, David?" Eve asked and tried not to wince when Mira's foot connected with hers.

"Maine. I used to live in Boston, which is where I'm originally from. The Maine house has been in my family since it was built over a hundred years ago. I'd always spent my vacations there and when it came to me, I decided to live there permanently."

Not far from Rock-Maine Island. They were practically neighbors...

"This is my first time on a cruise. My daughter's been trying to talk me into it for a while now. She finally wore me down."

"I hope you're enjoying yourself," Eve offered as Mira continued to be short on conversation, probably because all her other senses had been engaged.

"My daughter wanted me to get out and meet new people," he said. "No regrets so far." He fixed his twinkling blue gaze on Mira.

Eve knew she'd become invisible. However, they had business to take care of.

"How much did Jack tell you?" she asked.

David Bergstrom gave her a brief rundown. "The death occurred before the ship reached international waters so this actually falls under the jurisdiction of the NYPD but the FBI will most likely step in."

"I hope I didn't imagine any of it."

He shook his head. "The blunt force trauma didn't happen by itself."

It took a moment for her to respond. He really did have lovely eyes. Gentle. Pensive. "What I don't understand is why the captain is not taking measures to have the matter investigated."

"It's not unusual for a captain to come under pressure from the cruise ship bosses," David said distractedly. "It's a messy business. On board crimes reported are rarely prosecuted for lack of evidence or witnesses. In this case, however, we have the medical examiner's report to go on with. There's enough proof to suggest the victim met with foul play. The ship's legal team will likely argue the injury happened on impact when the body hit the water, but the examiner insists a weapon was used. It would be good if we could find something to collaborate the findings."

If only he could add a sense of urgency to his tone, Eve thought. Then again, no one was going anywhere. "Jack said you'd be working as a consultant. How much power does that give you?" Eve asked.

"I'm a civilian so I have to tread with care. I'll be examining the crime scene and identifying useful evidence. Also, I'll work on identifying likely suspects."

Apart from the other Carmen Miranda impersonators on board, Eve couldn't imagine who else would be capable of murder or have a reason for it. "Out of curiosity, where were you between eleven and midday yesterday?" Eve had tried to return the suitcase close to midday and the victim had been on the top deck at eleven when she'd taken the photo so she'd been killed soon after.

David gave her a small smile. "I was touring the ship with a group. There are pictures to prove it."

Mira kicked her under the table again. Eve grimaced. "Good. I'm glad we cleared that up."

David cleared his throat. "I understand you went to the victim's cabin at midday. Did she happen to be the one who shoved you out of the way?"

Eve couldn't remember telling Jack about that... "Touché." She got her cell phone out and called Jill. When she answered, Eve growled softly. "Did you tell Jack about our conversation?"

"It was for your own good, Eve," Jill said. "He wanted to know every detail about it. I know it sounds disloyal, but at least now you don't need to worry. Jack didn't suspect you but he wanted to make sure you'd be in the clear so he needed to know everything. He's got your back, Eve."

"Makes me wonder what else you tell him because you think it'll be for my own good," she whispered.

"Sorry, I didn't get any of that."

"I have to go. This call is costing me a fortune. My cell phone's switched over to the ship's satellite." She took a long sip of her coffee. "Well then, that's settled. Neither one of us killed her. So what's the plan, David?"

"Let the man have his breakfast first, Eve."

Chapter Four

DAVID BERGSTROM THANKED the purser for opening the cabin for them and then gestured for Eve to precede him. Eve relished the moment. Normally, she had to listen to Jack issuing his warnings to steer clear of any involvement.

"For an ex law enforcement officer, you're surprisingly relaxed and open-minded."

The edge of his lip kicked up. "Let me guess. You've been snooping around Jack's crime scenes and getting underfoot."

"Not intentionally."

"How did you two meet?" he asked.

Eve's gaze danced around the room. "At a crime scene. I inadvertently became the prime suspect." Eve decided Mira would love David's chuckle. It sounded throaty. Male. And delightfully playful.

"I'm now thinking you had him running around in circles."

She shrugged. "Again, not intentionally."

This time his chest shook. "I'd give anything to have been there."

"So where do you know him from?" she asked.

"It's actually a small world. We've crossed paths a few times. In fact, he worked one of his first cases with me."

"And then you taught him all you know?"

He nodded. "I also learned a few tricks along the way."

Modest to boot. She couldn't wait to tell Mira.

She knew her aunt had enjoyed a few special relationships, but none had evolved into something more serious and Eve had never really delved, so she didn't know how her aunt felt about marriage. Mira had close male friends, one in particular came to mind, Patrick McKenzie. To his dismay, Mira had never hinted at wanting anything more than friendship from him.

The fact Mira appeared to be moonstruck over David Bergstrom made Eve want to find out as much as she could about the man to make sure he'd do right by her.

"Take a moment to compare what you see now to what you saw yesterday," he suggested.

Eve thought she'd struggle to recall all details but she'd been trained as a chef and had an excellent memory, at least, for recipes. Although, she could also find her way around her kitchen blindfolded, as she always knew where everything was. She had a particular talent with becoming familiar with new kitchens—a trait she'd picked up during all those working vacations she'd taken.

David produced a professional looking camera and began taking photos of the cabin.

"Did you just happen to have that handy?"

He smiled. "No, I borrowed this from the cruise ship photographer."

Eve remained by the door and tried to think back to when she'd first nudged it open the previous day. She'd noticed some clothes and the fruit scattered on the floor. Everything she now saw seemed to match her mental inventory, but had any of it been moved? She didn't think so.

"Is it coming back to you?"

"I stood here and followed the trail of fruit. Then I lifted my gaze and looked out onto the balcony." She closed her eyes for a moment. "That's when I saw the scarf."

"What scarf?"

"It was hanging on the railing. Once I got my feet to respond, I rushed out and instinctively looked down. When I saw the body I rushed back inside to call for help. I..." She frowned. Had she grabbed the scarf on her way back in? She looked around the room. "I don't see the scarf anywhere. I guess it must have blown away." How much could she remember about the scarf?

The color green came to mind... with splashes of blue and purple.

"Do you notice anything else missing?"

"Everything I saw seems to be here. Should we check her personal effects... in case someone came in and helped themselves to something they thought the victim would no longer need?" The thought of theft of a dead person's belongings brought a bad taste to her mouth. If the scene remained undisturbed, all her personal possessions should be there. Handbag. Purse. Cell phone...

"We should stick to facts. I'm only asking you to recall what you know you saw. If something you know for a fact should be here, but isn't, then we'll know for sure someone took it."

She hummed under her breath. "So are you suggesting the scarf might have been removed?" And if so, why?

"You're certain you saw it?"

She nodded. "On the railing."

David strode over to the railing. "Jack left out a crucial bit of information."

"Why am I not surprised?"

"The victim suffered the blow to the front of the head." He stepped back from the railing and looked around. "The killer might have grabbed something from the room, or..." he brushed his hand across his chin, "The killer might have bashed the victim's head against the railing and then used the scarf to wipe any trace of blood."

Eve grimaced. Had David just pictured the scene in his mind? "But why would the killer then leave the scarf hanging on the railing?"

David shrugged. "Perhaps someone came into the room and the killer had to hide."

Eve's lips parted. "Are you suggesting—" She swirled around. Had the killer hidden under the bed or the bathroom while she'd been in the room?

"Yes, it's possible you were in the room at the same time as the killer."

"Hang on." She frowned. "If that's the case, that means the woman I saw coming out of the cabin is not the killer."

She closed her eyes and tried to recall if she'd maybe... smelled something. Perfume? Cologne? Aftershave lotion? Eve growled softly. The door to the balcony had been open. She could only remember smelling the sea breeze.

He gave her a pat on the shoulder. "You're doing well. Half the people I know would have run for their lives by now."

Eve didn't move. The realization of how close she might have been to the killer felt like a bucket of icy cold water had been thrown on her face. "Don't be fooled. My knees are knocking together." She looked around the room. There were some smooth surfaces. "Is there any way you could dust for prints?"

David chuckled. "Do I look like MacGyver to you?"

Eve lifted her chin. "You could use the lead from a pencil and some tape to lift off a print."

"And you think that would stand up in court?"

"A print is a print. At least it would point the finger at someone. It would be a start. As it is, we only have ninety-nine Carmen Miranda impersonators to suspect."

"Or anyone else the victim might have crossed paths with."

"What do you mean?"

"Anyone on board this cruise ship could be the killer. A deranged passenger. One of the crewmembers. She might have argued with one of the crew. That alone paves the way for possible motives. Imagine if a crew member got on her bad side and she threatened to complain about them."

"Would that be motive for murder?"

"Push a person too far and who knows what they'll do. Situations can flare up and get out of control even between people who've only just met or... it might have been an ongoing dispute. There are endless possibilities. It's our job to narrow them down. We should find out if she traveled on this ship before."

"This is the groups' tenth year anniversary. This could be the same cruise they went on in previous years." Eve gazed at the railing. "Who would be desperate enough to push someone over?"

"Try not to think about it too much."

"I can't help wondering what would drive a person to deliberately end someone else's life."

He brushed his hand across his chin. "Anger. There might have been an argument. The killer might have lost all control and acted on the spur of the moment."

"It's strange but I don't actually find that at all disconcerting. I'm more worried about someone doing this intentionally. A crime of passion or anger might plunge the perpetrator into a state of remorse. Whereas a premeditated act would mean there's a person who could plan something and see it through to completion without breaking into a sweat." She tried to clear the thought away but it refused to budge. "If the killer thinks I know something, what's to stop him... or her from coming after me?"

After they collected as much evidence as they could get, which only included the photographs David took, they made their way to the upper deck. The cabin would remain sealed and off limits to the cleaning staff. Hopefully, once the police boarded the ship they might be able to lift some prints. Something they could use to lead them to a suspect.

David disappeared for a moment and returned shortly with a colorful glass. "Make yourself inconspicuous. I'm going to do the rounds. See if I can engage with any of the anniversary people."

"Who?"

"The Carmen Miranda group."

"Oh, right." She swirled the cocktail umbrella around and took a sip. "It's fruit juice."

"You need to keep a clear head. Especially if you're standing anywhere near a railing."

As she sipped her drink, Eve took mental snap shots of the passengers strolling by. News about the death hadn't spread. The captain had made sure of that. He'd told her he would only be informing the passengers who'd come on board with the victim, meaning all the impersonators were in the know and had been asked to keep it all under wraps so as not to ruin everyone else's vacation.

Moments later, David strode back toward her, a happy smile on his face.

"This is their third consecutive time on this cruise ship."

"Fast work. Who gave you that information?"

"The purple Miranda." He signaled toward the opposite end of the deck to a group of them.

They all appeared to be chatting as if they were the best of friends but after the brief encounters she'd had with them Eve knew better. Those full-lipped smiles weren't fooling her.

"You realize what this means?"

Unfortunately, she did. "The net has widened to include the crew-members." Three trips on the same cruise ship. They'd become regulars. She finished her drink. Adjusting her sunglasses, she gazed out to sea and the clear blue sky. It all looked so calm. If she could stay in this moment for a bit longer...

"Do you have any suggestions on how to proceed?" she asked.

"You've done your part."

"What? I can't be excluded now."

"If something happens to you, Jack will hunt me down and I don't think I'd be able to outrun him."

"What he doesn't know won't hurt him." Eve mentally rolled up her sleeves.

If you want to hear the latest news, go to a hair salon and chat with the hairdresser. They're trained professionals in the art of conversation and listening, Eve thought as she rested her head against the basin and closed her eyes. She liked nothing better than having her hair washed and trying new products that always made her hair feel silky smooth. For Eve, this was the next best thing to taking a vacation.

"Have you ever thought about cutting it short?" the hairdresser asked as she rinsed her hair.

Amanda had been with this cruise ship for two years. In that time, Eve thought she must have crossed paths with the victim, but would she sacrifice her hair for information?

"It's short enough."

"Are you sure?" Amanda covered her head with a towel and began gently rubbing it dry. "You'd look cute with a pixie cut. It's my specialty."

"Just a blowout today, thanks." And information, she thought.

Amanda guided her to the chair. Eve declined the offer of a drink thinking David had been right and she really needed to keep a clear head.

"Does anyone from the Carmen Miranda group come to your salon?"

"A few. Why do you ask?"

"I've yet to see their hair. They're all wearing turbans."

Amanda looked around and then leaned in to whisper, "There's been a spike in appointments from them. Suddenly they all want their hair done."

"Any particular reason?"

"You haven't heard?" Amanda whispered.

"What?" Eve mouthed.

"Don't tell anyone you heard it from me, but one of them went overboard. Word is she jumped."

"Really?" She did her best to sound astonished. "And you think they're all coming to get their hair done because..."

"Therapy. Someone they know died. A couple of them came in person to make their bookings and they looked stressed out. It all affects your hair."

It did? "So people are actually saying she jumped?"

Amanda nodded.

"Anyone in particular?"

Amanda took a moment to think about it. "That's strange. They all seemed to mention it."

Almost as if by mutual agreement? Had they all decided to spread the rumor to divert any suspicion away from them?

"What possible reason would she have to take her own life?"

"Who knows?"

Give it your best shot, Eve thought. "She must have had problems."

"Maybe, but I doubt they were money problems. She could afford the cruise every year."

Had she pushed her credit limit? Eve considered brainstorming the idea but then she shook her head. They'd already decided she'd been killed.

"Or maybe she got mixed up with the wrong crowd," Amanda added. "A lot of funny business goes on. Passengers come on board a cruise ship, but they're none the wiser. All sorts of under the table transactions go on. Whatever you need, you can get."

It took a moment for Eve to engage her brain. "Drugs?" Eve mouthed.

Amanda nodded. "Not that I'd know anything about any of it. I only took this job because my cousin Leanne ran off with my fiancé and I couldn't afford to run the beauty salon we had by myself. Bills started piling up. In the end, I had to pack it all in. I figured I needed a working holiday and someone suggested I try a cruise ship..."

Eve pretended to listen attentively; all the while her mind churned the information Amanda had provided. What sort of racket were they running on this ship? And how would a passenger get involved? Trafficking? Selling?

Amanda talked about her experience working on the cruise ship and the people she'd met along the way. Eve nodded even though she couldn't hear much of what Amanda said over the hairdryer.

She'd never been one to sit still and watch the hairdresser perform her magic, so her attention drifted.

Photographs were pinned around the mirror. They were party shots, but from where she sat she could barely make out the details. Then she caught sight of a turban with what looked to be cherries and a pineapple on it.

She narrowed her gaze and tried to lean in as far as she could.

Amanda tapped her shoulder and pointed at the photo. "That's her. The dead woman. Crystal Reid. She had an appointment for today. When she made the booking, she said she needed something special for a special occasion with a special someone. It broke my heart to have to cross her name off."

Had she been planning a rendezvous with someone? A woman's interest in her personal appearance tended to spike when there was a man involved...

"Did she mention anyone in particular?"

"Why do you ask?"

Eve didn't want to raise Amanda's suspicions. "If she planned on meeting with a man then that means there's someone on board grieving. I wouldn't want to say anything to upset anyone."

Amanda held her gaze for a few seconds and then shook her head. "Sorry, I can't help you."

Eve noticed Amanda pressed her lips and turned her focus to the task at hand.

She was hiding something...

"You should drink chamomile tea to soothe the nerves," the masseuse suggested. "Oh, dear. I found another knot. Just relax."

Easier said than done. Eve focused on her breathing. Her nose twitched. The scent of Jasmine and something else she couldn't identify wafted around her. "There must be something in the air. I swear I felt relaxed when I came on board and then... something happened," she said over the sound of waves lapping gently against the shore recording playing in the background.

"You must have picked up a vibe."

"That could be it. Have you heard any bad news?" Eve asked.

The masseuse stopped for a moment and appeared to think about it.

"You have." Eve raised her head slightly.

"We're not supposed to talk about it."

And yet human nature would prevail. "It would help to know so I can focus on getting rid of the feeling." Eve sighed under her breath and dropped her head back as the smooth strokes worked their magic.

"There was an incident, but nothing that should really affect the passengers."

"Was it something violent? It must have been because I don't react well to those. I saw a street fight once and I swear I couldn't move my neck for a week after that. I felt so stressed..."

"You must be hyper-sensitive."

"One with the universe, that's me." It's what Jill would say, Eve thought. "If there's a disturbance, I pick up on it straight away."

"You mean the way birds can sense earthquakes before they hit?"

"Yes, something like that. It runs in the family. My granny never had to check the weather forecast. She always knew when a storm was approaching." Eve knew her real granny, who insisted she use her full name, would give her a roll of her eyes.

"I really shouldn't tell you this... but... someone went overboard."

"No. Really?" So the captain had sanitized the death.

"Crystal Reid. She was one of my regular customers. Last year she came in with a serious complaint about her neck. It turned out she'd been wearing a real pineapple on her head and all the effort to keep it balanced strained her neck."

"Now that I think about it, I've heard her name mentioned."

"In what context? Hope it wasn't someone speaking ill of the dead. That never bodes well."

"No. Someone mentioned she'd been talking about the rendezvous she'd been planning with someone really special. I'm guessing she had a date lined up."

"I wouldn't know about that."

Going by the pressure the masseuse applied on her shoulder, Eve suspected she'd clammed up.

Out of loyalty?

To whom?

Someone higher up. Someone wielding control over the crew. One of the officers would tick the box but anyone in a position of authority could use it to give people the incentive to do as they were told. Especially if they were running some sort of racket on board.

Chapter Five
_____

"SHE KNEW THE KILLER," Eve declared as she burst into the cabin.

Both Mira and David looked up. The delayed reaction told Eve they'd been deep in conversation and were most likely still thinking about what they'd been murmuring to each other. Their eyes looked slightly glazed over as if they'd been lost in each other's gaze.

Mira... In love? So soon?

"Come join us. We're having coffee,"

"How about I come back later?" Eve suggested.

Mira rolled her eyes.

There were only two chairs out on the balcony. That meant she'd have to lean against the railing. Her theories could wait...

"You can pull up a chair and sit by the door," Mira suggested.

A fair compromise.

"Your hair looks lovely," David said.

A man complimenting a woman's hair...

More brownie points.

"Thank you. I only had it washed but for a moment there I thought I might have to agree to a haircut so the hairdresser would open up," she said and caught them up on her findings.

"So you think the impersonators are trying to spread the rumor she jumped. What if it's true? They knew her best."

"No. I'm convinced they're trying to cover something up. They're probably protecting someone." She brushed her hands across her face.

"Hard day?" Mira asked lightly.

"You said coming on a cruise would do me a world of good. I've just had a massage and I'm already tense."

"David, we need to get this sorted out before Eve cracks up."

"Go ahead, have fun at my expense."

Out of the corner of her eye, she saw Mira exchange a look with David that spoke of resignation. Mira knew her best. Eve wouldn't let this go...

"So why do you think she knew the killer?" Mira asked.

"How else would the killer gain access to her cabin? It would make sense for the killer to be someone she knew or was involved with." She shrugged. "If it's not someone from the Carmen Miranda group, perhaps she was having a clandestine affair. The man might be married. I have no idea how we'll identify him. Both the hairdresser and masseuse clammed up on me. That alone makes me suspicious." She drew in a deep breath and rolled her shoulders.

"So you shifted your suspicions from the impersonators to a lover because the hairdresser alluded to a rendezvous."

Eve knew Mira was now trying to humor her, and with good reason. A few month's before, she'd come close to holding the entire island under suspicion. "It's a lead. At least, I think it is." Her voice sounded halfhearted. She leaned back and closed her eyes.

"It could just be a coincidence."

Eve shook her head. "A coincidence is Jack finding out there is a detective on board the ship and... not just any detective, but one Jack knows from way back."

David smiled. "Don't mention I told you, but Jack was seriously thinking about finding a way to come on board but he changed his mind when he came across his first grade teacher's name on the passenger list."

His first grade teacher? Eve made a mental note to find out more...

"Anyway, you might be onto something," David suggested. "The love interest might be Carlos Bradbury."

"Carlos?"

"It's actually Charles. He's a musical theatre director who joins the Carmen Miranda group on their cruises. It's a sort of working vacation for him. He helps them out with their choreography."

The more she thought about it, the more she wanted to believe one of the impersonators had allowed jealousy to get the better of them. Yes, a crime of passion that involved jealousy would make sense... and put her at ease. If this turned out to be a carefully contrived plan to commit murder, she'd never be able to sleep easy. "He's probably the man I saw bringing the Carmen Miranda group to heel." Eve nibbled the edge of her lip. "That paves the way for another theory. I got the impression all the ladies had their eyes on him. If Crystal had managed to snag him—"

"Sorry to interrupt, but who's Crystal?" Mira asked.

"The victim. And that reminds me. Jack never mentioned her name. Surely he must know it."

David gave a small nod.

"Why would Jack withhold her name?" Eve couldn't help thinking it had been a deliberate omission. As soon as the victim's identity had been established, the name should have tripped off his tongue...

"He's not keen on you becoming involved," David explained.

"But he said—"

"To keep your eyes open and ears to the ground," David nodded.

"He was humoring me." Eve huffed out a breath. "He can be so infuriating."

"You don't know the half of it."

"I wouldn't be surprised to learn he'd tried to have the ship turn back so I could get off it."

David grinned. "He tried, but the captain refused saying he'd received orders from the top to keep going."

"I'm surprised he shared the medical examiner's findings with me."

"Oh, that was meant to put you off. And it worked for a while. Mira tells me you refused to leave your cabin." David gave her an encouraging pat on the back. "Don't worry about it. I appreciate your input. You did well. Now we know there are two crew members who know something."

"I'm sure they're withholding vital information," Eve said.

"Perhaps I could try to get something more out of them," Mira suggested. "It might look too suspicious if you try again, Eve."

Both Eve and David shook their heads. "Out of the question. You can't get involved in this, Mira."

Her aunt didn't argue. "So have either of you thought of motives?"

"You sound just like Jack."

"He's not around, so someone has to."

They all sat in silence for a moment.

Eve was about to suggest they take a break when she sat up. "Okay. We know Crystal was meeting with someone and she had made an appointment at the hair salon. She wanted to look her best for a lover. What if someone else had their eye on him? They might have taken steps to stop Crystal. They confronted her. They warned her to back off. When she refused, the argument escalated and it got out of hand."

"I'm impressed. Next time I get stuck with my story, I'm going to use you as my sounding board, Eve."

David laughed. "You've got it in for the impersonators."

"They did this to themselves." Eve shrugged. "They're not the nicest people. Their aggressive behavior has made them suspects."

David thought about it for a minute. "It sounds plausible."

Eve turned to her aunt. "Mira? Is that a good enough motive for you?"

Mira gave her a small smile. "It's a start."

"How do we follow this up?" she asked and hoped David had forgotten about excluding her.

"Divide and conquer," David suggested. "If we speak to the impersonators separately, one of them might give someone else away."

Eve sighed.

"What's wrong?"

"Well, I'm not sure they'll open up. I think they're covering for someone and that's why they're spreading the rumor Crystal jumped."

"But you can't be sure."

She slumped back on her chair. "Okay. You'll have to use your charm on them, David. I get the feeling they don't like me."

"It has to be one of them," Mira said. "Didn't you say the hairdresser told you they were all rushing in for appointments? Now Crystal is out of the way, they want to cease the opportunity. And that means the love interest has to be Carlos. Going by what you saw, he has them all under his thumb."

"If that's the case, the killer might be ruthless enough to keep getting rid of her competition." Eve groaned under her breath. "Now I'm thinking Carlos could be the killer." She made a helpless gesture. "David, how on earth do the police do it?"

"They find evidence and support it with motive and opportunity, and they consider all possible scenarios. If they put enough pressure on the right person, they're bound to crack."

She raised a finger. "One. We need to know what Carlos was getting up to between eleven and midday. Right after I saw him breaking up the fight." It sounded like a solid first step. Eve raised another finger. "Two. After the scuffle on deck, Crystal returned to her cabin. Then... someone followed her. It would help to know who."

David smiled but Eve could tell he wanted to laugh.

"Yes, that would really help," he agreed.

Eve clicked her fingers. "Security cameras. Why

didn't we think of those before? Actually, Mira... you mentioned them."

"I was only thinking of the cameras installed on some ships to detect anyone going overboard. I think it became law to install them. But you're right. They must have them around inside the ship."

David's jaw muscles tensed.

Eve could sense him wondering how he'd missed it. He surged to his feet and strode back inside the cabin and made a beeline for the door. Moments later, he returned.

"Yes. They're inconspicuous but they're there. I suppose no one notices them because they've come on the cruise to enjoy themselves."

"Do you think we can gain access to the footage?"

Mira had opened up her laptop. After a brief read of a few articles, she looked up and shook her head. "According to this article the cruise lines tend to protect their own employee's legal interests, not the passenger's rights. In some criminal cases, the cruise lines destroy evidence and sanitize the crime scene. I guess we're lucky they haven't done that."

Eve sat forward. "Not yet."

"This goes on to say criminals on cruise ships are rarely prosecuted."

"Don't they have security people... someone... anyone to keep the peace?"

Mira pointed to the laptop screen. "Unlike airplanes with federal marshals, cruise ships have no police authorities aboard. They do, however, have security guards, but they're loyal to their employer, not to the passenger."

"What is that suppose to mean?"

"Your guess is as good as mine. For what it's worth, I think they'll try anything to avoid litigation."

"If I'd known that before, I doubt I would have agreed to come, Mira. I still can't believe they don't have personnel on ships to deal with possible crimes."

Mira tapped the screen again. "They do follow procedure. Cruise lines respond by notifying their risk management departments and their defense lawyers. No doubt they'll be boarding at the next port."

"A lot of good that'll do the victim. Just as well we're here. Otherwise, the killer would get away with murder."

Both David and Mira looked at her in silence.

Eve gave a firm nod. "Yes, I'm committed to doing as much as I possibly can to point the finger of suspicion at someone. When the ship docks, the police can take over. This crime can't go unpunished."

"She sounds offended," David said.

Mira nodded.

"Do you blame me? I came on this cruise to relax and look at me, I'm a nervous wreck." She turned to David. "Do you think you can gain access to the video footage?"

Mira sighed.

"Let me guess. If they find anything incriminating, they'll tape over it and get rid of the evidence."

"Sorry, Eve. This article is not the only inflammatory one."

"Those articles must have been written by victims of crime. I have a good mind to... to ask you, Mira, to write something."

Mira shook her head. "You're not going to like this one."

"Read it out loud, please."

"A few years back, a cruise line hired a top notch company to carry out a study. After extensive analysis, the experts concluded that misconduct occurred frequently during cruises. Apparently, most crew members were not afraid of being arrested, much less convicted due to lack of evidence. I'm sure things have changed now."

Eve sat up. "Well, if they haven't, they're in for a rude awakening."

"Then there's this other article which states that cruise ships are floating cities with all the security needs of normal cities. See, that's reassuring."

Nothing but lip service, Eve thought. "Apart from questioning me, the captain hasn't lifted a finger to open an investigation. We need to pursue this ourselves. David, you're the only one with any real authority, so you'll have to gain access to the videos."

"Is she always this bossy?" he asked chuckling.

Mira gave a small nod. "You're lucky. She asked

nicely. I've seen her in action in the kitchen. She can be quite ferocious."

"Hey, I'm nice to my staff."

"Then why do you yell at them?"

"How else are they going to hear me over all the noise? Besides, they get to yell right back at me."

"I'll have a word with the captain." David rose to his feet and excused himself. "We'll catch up at dinner, ladies."

Eve barely waited for the door to close before turning to Mira. "I think he's annoyed he didn't think about the security cameras. Hope I didn't wound his pride."

"He's bigger than that." Mira's tone carried admiration.

"So, tell me all."

Mira gave her a brisk smile. "There's nothing to tell."

"Oh, come on. You like him."

"How can I not like him? He's read my books."

"Yes, but... you really like him."

"You sound like a teenager."

"And you're acting like one. Which is great. I've never seen your eyes sparkle."

"I can't help feeling he's a fictional character come to life."

"In other words, a dream come true?"

"Yes."

Mira's uncharacteristic dreamy tone caught Eve by

surprise. Maybe something wonderful would come out of this cruise after all.

"I'm going to try do get some writing done before lunch. Promise me you won't antagonize anyone, Eve. Remember, this is a cruise ship. There's nowhere to run."

Chapter Six

WHAT? I'm on vacation, Eve silently hollered when she made eye contact with a woman who, going by the curl of her lip, clearly disapproved of her appearance.

What could possibly be wrong with a pair of white shorts and t-shirt? She'd thought it would help her blend in so she wouldn't look so conspicuous when she set off on her reconnaissance mission.

A passenger came out of his cabin and hung a Do Not Disturb sign on the door.

"Maybe that's what I should do in our cabin," Eve murmured. Or she could hang it around her neck. Do Not Disturb or Kill...

Turning a corner, she huffed out a breath. Great. Several Carmen Miranda impersonators were headed her way.

No doubt they'd think she was making a statement and turning her nose up at their multi-colored clothes.

Eve stepped out of the way of one before she plowed her down, the rhythm of her walk suggesting if Eve didn't take a sideways step, she'd do just that.

Eve played around with the idea of making light of the moment and engaging the woman in conversation but that task had fallen on David. With his charm and good looks he stood a better chance of extricating something worthwhile from them.

When she reached Crystal's cabin, she slowed down and looked over her shoulder straight at the camera at the end of the corridor.

If David could get his hands on the video footage, this would all be wrapped up in no time.

Seeing a woman trotting toward her from the opposite direction, Eve dug her hands inside her pockets and pretended to search for something. The woman waved at her.

"Running late for my bridge game."

She wore white Bermuda shorts, a pink and purple blouse and a thick gold necklace that disappeared into her voluptuous cleavage. Eve tried to disregard the fake lashes and tan. She watched her toddle off in her high-heeled sandals and waited for her to disappear before making her move.

Looking around her, she tested the door handle. Locked. As she moved away from Crystal's cabin, someone came out of the neighboring cabin. A woman wearing an oversized straw hat. Thankfully with no fruit on it. As she turned, she made eye contact with Eve and smiled. Eve wondered if she should ask her if she'd heard anything, but most passengers had been up on deck enjoying their first day out at sea.

"Is your friend all right?" the woman asked.

"Friend?" Eve asked.

"Oh, I thought you just came out of the cabin next door."

"No, I was passing through. Was there something wrong with the passenger?"

The woman lowered her voice. "I couldn't help overhearing the arguments."

Arguments?

The woman put her hand to her chest. "The second one was worse than the first."

"What were the arguments about?"

"I only picked up a few words. Liar. Cheat. And a few others, which don't bear repeating. I'll never understand why people come on vacation and bring their anger with them. No consideration for others."

"Did you say you heard a couple of arguments?"

The woman nodded and adjusted her hat. "I thought the one with the woman would end badly. They screeched and hissed. It was all dreadfully upsetting. I held my stomach."

"I would have too," Eve offered. "What about the other one?" she asked as they strode along the corridor.

"Oh, I could only hear her voice, but I heard the man clear his throat. That's how I know it was a man. The door slamming was just as bad as the arguing. People coming and going."

"More than two?"

"I'm not sure. The sleeping tablet I took on the flight over left me feeling fuzzy headed and I was dozing off. I'm from Seattle and my daughter moved to New York last year so I try to visit once a year. This time, she surprised me with a cruise and whizzed me straight from the airport to the cruise terminal, and here I am..."

"That was a lovely gesture."

The woman smiled. "My daughter is pushing me to get out and about and find someone new but I've been a widow for too long. I'm happy with my life. Besides, it's a bit late for me. By the way, I'm Joanna."

Eve berated herself for thinking Joanna's daughter might have simply wanted to get her out of the way. Then she thought of her own mother... Her stomach muscles clenched. She imagined her mother calling to say she planned on visiting. Perhaps next Christmas she could suggest they all go on a cruise together and Eve could bail out at the last minute...

"Lovely to meet you, I'm Eve. And, for what it's worth, it's never too late for love or companionship." The woman looked to be older than Mira, perhaps in her early seventies, but Eve had heard of plenty of people in their golden years finding love again. "So after the argument with the man you didn't hear anything else?"

"Maybe she had the argument with the man first," Joanna said as they came up to the elevator.

"Either way, you have extremely good hearing."

"Oh, I was sitting on the balcony. They must have had their balcony door open. When it got too much, I moved back inside and closed the door."

Eve's excitement over finding a possible witness fizzled as the woman clearly couldn't recall which argument she'd heard last.

When the elevator doors opened, Joanna stepped inside but Eve hesitated.

"Coming?"

"Actually, I think I left something behind. Lovely meeting you and enjoy the rest of your cruise," Eve said as the elevator doors swished closed. She stood there a moment and wondered how she could find out if anyone else had heard the arguments.

While it would all be resolved when David got his hands on the video footage, it would help to have more solid information to collaborate whatever they found in the video. Thinking that if she'd managed to bump into one of the neighbors, she might encounter another, Eve doubled back.

As she again walked past Crystal's cabin, she had a brilliant idea and knocked on the cabin next door. A young woman answered. Her long hair hung loosely around her shoulders and Eve could tell she'd been in the process of drying it.

"Oh, I must have the wrong cabin," Eve said, her tone all innocence and apologetic.

"Who were you after?" she asked, her tone crisp.

"I met this lovely woman who said she'd been having trouble sleeping because of the neighbor and I wanted to know how she was getting on." Not exactly the truth, but neither was it a lie.

The young woman rolled her eyes and pointed to the cabin next to hers. Crystal's cabin.

"I know exactly what she was talking about. Yesterday, I tried to get some shuteye... I had a farewell party before boarding and then there were the welcoming drinks. I really needed a few minutes to doze off, but all I could hear was this incessant bickering."

"Really? How dreadful. Is it a couple?"

"Hard to say. At first I thought it was two women and then I heard a man's voice. Maybe it was a tryst." She edged the door to close it.

"Well, sorry to have bothered you. I'll try the cabin on the other side."

"Now that I think about it, she had more than one man in there."

"At the same time?"

"No, at least I don't think so. Like I said, I was trying to get some shuteye. Anyway, all's good now. I haven't heard a peep from her."

"Good to hear. Again, sorry to have bothered you. I'll try the next cabin." Eve strode off. Sensing the young woman still watching her, she stopped at Joanna's door and knocked. After a minute, she looked over her shoulder at the young woman. Shrugging, Eve moved on.

Two men visited Crystal...

They'd been struggling to identify one man. Now they had two to contend with.

Eve crossed her fingers and hoped David came through with the goods. Meanwhile, she decided to resume her mission. Stake out the joint. If she hovered around long enough, she was bound to hear something, and what better place than the restaurants. She'd start at one end of the ship and work her way through.

"On a diet?"

Eve had just hit her tenth buffet thinking that if anyone had heard about Crystal's death, they might be talking about it and with any luck, she'd overhear the conversation. In order to maintain her cover of innocent bystander, she'd played the role to the hilt by eating as many meals as she could. To a normal... regular person, she knew her modus operandi wouldn't make sense. But it had been all she could think of doing to make herself look inconspicuous.

She looked down at her helping of Caesar Salad. It would only take one mouthful for her zipper to burst, so she'd have to play around with this one.

"I'm saving my appetite for dinner." And she'd most likely have to be rolled there.

"The trick is to wear loose pants and to go for a walk between servings."

"I'll keep that in mind."

The man looked to be in his thirties. Good looking in a boy next door way. Without being too judgmental, Eve thought he'd be better looking if he dropped a few pounds...

"And always leave room for dessert," he suggested, "But I suppose someone as skinny as you doesn't have to worry about that."

"You'd be surprised." She glanced around for a table and spotting one, made a beeline for it. When she settled down, she looked up.

"Mind if I join you? The place's filled up quickly."

In that split second, Eve had to decide if she'd just acquired a stalker. "Sure."

"I'm Bronson Charles. Yes, like the movie star but in reverse. My dad was a huge fan." He sat down in front of her and bit into a French fry.

"I'm Eve Lloyd."

They both sat in silence for a few minutes, each one casting furtive glances around.

Yes, a diamond in the rough, Eve thought. Take away a few pounds and he might not have asked if he could join her because he would've been flocked by admiring women.

He looked around him and cringed. "I swear there's more bling here than in Vegas. An explosion of glitz, color, neon and gaudy art."

"I thought I was the only one who'd noticed."

"Have you been to the Star of the Sea lounge?"

Eve was almost afraid to ask. "What am I missing?"

"Fish tanks surround the entire area. Puts you right off ordering fish. I couldn't shake off the feeling they were eyeballing me."

"I'll keep that in mind." She pushed aside the few walnuts she'd encountered on her plate and stabbed a lettuce leaf.

"Traveling alone?"

Her stalker alert beeped again. "No, I'm with a couple of other people."

His eyes danced around her face. "They ditch you?" he asked around a mouthful of fries.

"We're giving each other space." She had to take a bite of something.

He tilted his head. "Lloyd. The name rings a bell. Any relation to the author?"

"Yes. She's my aunt. How did you know about her?"

"It's in the program. She's reading an excerpt from her next novel."

"Are you a fan?" She expected him to laugh it off. Instead, he surprised her.

"Big fan. You wouldn't guess it by looking at me."

After her close calls with several killers on the island, Eve knew better than to judge a book by its cover. He had a handsome face. Bright eyes with a hint of mischief. He could probably stand to lose a few pounds, she insisted, but that was only her preference. Did he look like a man who read romances? No, she'd never have guessed it.

"I'm not judging."

He chortled. "I've been single for a couple of years now and not having much luck so I thought I'd think outside the box and try to figure out what women look for in a man. What better way to find out than to read the type of books that keep them going back for more?"

"Smart thinking. Have you discovered the secret?"

"There are all types of alpha males to choose from. I'm not sure I can pull off the brooding type and I don't have any hang-ups, so I'm veering toward the one with a twinkle in their eye that screams fun."

She didn't want to burst his bubble but even those heroes were usually described as well built with flat stomachs...

"I know what you're thinking." Bronson patted his slight pouch. "That's why I'm on this cruise. I've signed up for a full makeover. The personal trainer working with me promised to have me in tiptop shape by the time we sail into port. And yes, I could have joined a gym back home. In fact, I did. But there's always an excuse or something's always cropping up." He looked around. "I'm a captive audience here. If I don't rock up at the gym, the guy will hunt me down. He's committed."

Eve tried to avert her gaze, but it fell on his double-decker burger.

He chuckled. "I actually burn it up quickly. Thing is, I spent a few months in hospital after a car accident and all that lack of mobility piled up on me."

That made sense. "Here's a tip, Bronson."

"I'm all ears."

"You should walk the walk now. Whoever falls for you as you are, will love you no matter how you look. Imagine how much more they'll love you after you've burned off the excess weight."

"So I should let my sparkling charisma do all the work for me."

She nodded. "I have a friend who'd say you should act as if you're already the perfect weight."

"Good point. What are you doing for dinner tonight?"

Eve gave him a small smile. "I'm dining with those friends I mentioned. I'd ask you to join us but you might miss out on meeting that special person you're looking for. And... I have someone back home." She gave herself a small pat on the back for letting him down easy. She only hoped Bronson got the message.

"Maybe I'll meet someone at the reading. It'd be good to have something in common."

What were the chances of meeting two men who enjoyed reading Mira's books? Was there a new breed of men she didn't know about? Had Jack read Mira's books? And if he hadn't... would he?

Bronson chuckled under his breath. "Now I won't be able to get that tune out of my head."

"What tune?"

He nodded toward the stairs. "Chica chica boom boom chic. Every time I see them I think of the song."

A group of Carmen Miranda impersonators made their way to the buffet, clearly walking to the rhythm of some inner tune.

"I heard one of them jumped overboard."

Her mouth gaped open. "Where did you hear that?" No one was supposed to know.

"At breakfast. I went in there early and overheard some of the servers talking about it."

She'd suffered through all those meals and hadn't heard a single beep. "What else did they say?"

"It's strange. It actually sounded as if they were interrogating each other. Asking where they'd been at midday. Apparently, the captain put them all under the spotlight."

Interesting. Had the captain decided to launch his own investigation?

"Is something wrong?" he asked.

"Just thinking." If the captain had taken steps to question the crew that meant he hadn't found anything in the video footage. Or... he had found something, but it hadn't been enough to identify the perpetrator.

"So how are you entertaining yourself on the ship?"

"Huh?" she said distractedly.

Bronson laughed.

"Sorry." She cleared her throat. "Pardon?"

"I liked the huh better. Nothing wrong with huh." He smiled and shook his head. "Are you here to do nothing and relax or do you have a schedule of activities as some passengers seem to have."

"I came completely unprepared. Playing it by ear but... I should really knuckle down and do some work." She tilted her head and thought about her inn. If she couldn't relax, then she could at least begin working on her menu for the inn.

Eve told Bronson about her new business venture.

"So you don't have any experience running an inn but you can cook. That's half the problem solved. You can hire people to do the rest."

"I guess that's the general idea."

"I'm going to have to plan a weekend getaway to the island. Check out your inn. What's your selling point? You know, what will draw visitors to the island?"

Murder and mayhem?

No. They'd already had enough murder and mayhem on the island. It wouldn't happen again...

"Peace and quiet. The perfect place to spend a few days enjoying fine cuisine, long walks, horseback riding, the sights... There's fishing and hiking. And we have our own local celebrity. My aunt. Also, I have a friend who's interested in running some art classes. It should be fun. A local book club has already staked a claim on the front parlor for their weekly get together sessions and my aunt Mira will do some of her launches at the inn." Eve nibbled the edge of a lettuce leaf. "Yes, I really should use my time on the cruise to work on a menu."

"I'll definitely have to come." He looked away. "There they go again. Chica chica boom boom chic."

Don't look, Eve. Don't.

Eve couldn't help herself.

As she slanted her gaze toward the group of impersonators, they all turned toward her.

"Whoa. What did you do to deserve that? I swear they threw daggers at you."

Did they know something she didn't...?

Chapter Seven
_____

SEEING DAVID STRIDING TOWARD HER, Eve tried to hurry her step but her stomach gave a sharp protest so she mouthed, "The video footage?"

He gave her a small shake of his head and waited until he'd reached her to say more. "I was hoping you wouldn't ask."

Her heart sank. "Bad news?"

"We hit a dead end. The CCTV tapes have been erased."

"How can that be? It's only been a day."

David shrugged. "The captain said it's common practice to tape over them. The videos are on a loop and automatically record over themselves every day."

"So soon?" She didn't believe that for a minute. "I suspect the captain has already viewed them and he found something suspicious he doesn't want us to see."

"Do you have something to back up your suspicions?" David asked, "Other than your female intuition."

"Someone told me he overheard the servers complaining they'd been interrogated and asked to provide alibis. If the captain viewed the footage, he might have found reason to become suspicious of the crew. Otherwise, I'm sure he wouldn't have bothered questioning them."

David nudged her arm and guided her toward the elevator.

"Where are we going?"

"I'm going to have a chat with Carlos. His cabin is a few doors down from Crystal's. He might have seen or heard something. I overhead one of the Carmen Miranda impersonators say he's a regular at the Cabana Bar. I was on my way over there."

Eve could barely hide her surprise. "And you want me to come along?"

"As a diversionary tactic. When I approach him, I want you to stay in the background. You're with me but you won't join in the conversation. That way, he'll think you have nothing to do with my investigation. Since we can't avoid being seen together, we can pretend you have nothing to do with looking into the murder."

"Did Jack put you up to it?"

"I don't want to be the one to cause any friction between you two."

Eve laughed. "We tend to work around it."

"I'd sleep easier if I knew you weren't drawing unnecessary attention to yourself."

Eve slipped her hands inside her pockets. "Actually, I'm bound to draw attention whether I like it or not." As they stepped out of the elevator, she looked around. She didn't see anyone else wearing shorts and flip-flops. "I'm guessing they have a dress code."

"You look great. If anyone objects, they'll have to answer to me."

She smiled. "David Bergstrom, you're a regular champion."

"It's my super power."

"Most men would have ignored my remark. Or like Jack, used the opportunity to tell me to stay out of trouble. For instance, when I asked what I should pack for my cruise, he suggested I leave the gun and take the cannoli."

He laughed. "It'll be good to catch up with him."

If David planned on catching up with Jack, that meant he'd be visiting the island as well. She couldn't wait to tell Mira.

They had no trouble spotting Carlos Bradbury sitting at the bar dressed in white pants and a white shirt with his dark hair sleeked back.

David drew out a stool for Eve and took the one next to Carlos. He acknowledged him with a small nod and a remark about the pleasant weather they were all enjoying.

"Are you with the Carmen Miranda group?"

"What gave me away?" Carlos asked with a sparkling white smile that aimed at being charming but struck Eve as far too smooth to trust.

"I've seen you with them."

He nodded. "I've been working with the girls. They're putting on a show in a few days."

"They must be distraught over their loss."

"You know about it?"

"I'm assisting with the investigation."

"I didn't realize there was one."

David gave a small nod and produced a badge. Eve wondered if he could still flaunt it around.

Carlos sighed. "It was a dreadful blow to all of us. I had been working with Crystal on a solo number. No one knew about it." Carlos gave a small chuckle. "Actually, they're all working on a solo number. It's the prize for the winner of the competition."

"And are you helping everyone?"

Carlos made an open hand gesture. "There's only so much of me to go around. But I do my best."

"Who's taken Crystal's place? I assume your talents are in high demand and the gap she left has been snatched by someone else."

"That's still being decided."

A waiter approached them. Eve ordered an orange juice only to regret it when David ordered a beer.

"Who makes the decision?" David asked, his tone casual.

"I do, of course."

"Based on what?"

"Talent. What else?"

Bribery, Eve thought.

"They must all be bending over backward trying to impress you."

When Carlos laughed, Eve thought she heard an edge of nervousness in his tone.

"There's a healthy competitive spirit among them." Carlos contemplated the contents of his glass and then looked up at David. "I'm beginning to think you're interrogating me."

"When was the last time you spoke with Crystal Reid?" David asked almost as if to confirm the suspicion.

Carlos leaned slightly toward David. "I don't kiss and tell."

An admission!

He and Crystal had been lovers.

David had turned toward Carlos so from where she sat, Eve couldn't see the expression on his face but she imagined him giving Carlos a steady, unblinking look.

"I saw her briefly the day she died."

Surely he had to know she hadn't simply died. The captain had said he would inform the group. Eve assumed that also included telling them of the suspicious circumstances.

Had the words slipped out without much thought or had Carlos weighed each word, choosing the ones which would least implicate him in Crystal's death?

"What time?"

Carlos shrugged. "I'm on vacation and in no hurry to get anywhere so I don't bother wearing a watch."

Again, Eve suspected David had pinned him with his gaze.

"It would have been close to midday. After I saw her, I went for a stroll on the upper decks and saw people already heading to the restaurants for lunch."

Had he made a point of heading toward a public area where others could see him and, if necessary, verify his whereabouts?

"Then what did you do?"

"I wasn't hungry yet so I had a drink at the bar."

"Had Crystal been in a good mood?"

"Always. She had a sparkly personality."

That would eliminate the rumor making the rounds. Happy people did not commit suicide.

"And what did you talk about?"

"We discussed her dance routine steps. She wanted to make some last minute changes."

"And?"

"I told her I couldn't spare the time. She didn't like that."

"Did you argue?"

Carlos chuckled. "Us? No, never. We had an easy relationship. She respected my opinion and backed down."

"Just like that?"

"Oh, she might have tried to push harder."

"And how did she do that?"

Crystal's neighbor had said she'd heard Crystal arguing with a man but he hadn't raised his voice.

"As cheerful as she was, Crystal could be demanding. She already had my attention..."

"Your full attention?"

"I'm here to help all the contest participants so no one has an unfair advantage."

That seemed to contradict what he'd said moments before. Eve wondered if David's questions were getting to him.

"So she didn't get mad with you?"

It only took one person to lose their temper for a situation to escalate and perhaps get out of control.

"No."

"Not even a little?"

Carlos shifted in his seat.

"I don't wish to speak ill of the dead."

"But..."

"Crystal's sweetness had an edge. She was brought up pampered and could sometimes forget herself if she didn't get her own way."

"Did Crystal receive special attention from you?"

"As I said, she could be demanding."

David took a pensive drink of his beer.

Eve noticed the bartender hadn't moved from where he stood near them. She'd bet anything he was trying to overhear the conversation.

"Did anyone in particular resent her for that?" David asked.

"Hard to say when they all smile so sweetly."

Leaning against the mother of pearl counter, Eve looked up and gazed at the light fixtures sparkling like stars in a velvety blue sky. Carlos played the neutral card well. He wouldn't give anyone away or say anything to incriminate himself.

"You said you saw her close to midday on the day she died. Did Crystal invite you to her cabin?"

Eve leaned back in time to see Carlos take a nervous swallow.

"Yes."

"When did she invite you?"

"When I went up to the upper deck, and just as well I did."

"Why?"

"They had all promised they wouldn't dress up on the first day, but no one kept their promise. I knew it wouldn't take long for sparks to fly. I got there in time to break up a fight."

"How did you take control of the situation?"

"I threatened to walk out on all of them, so they all promised to behave. As I strode off, Crystal asked me to go see her."

Had someone overheard her?

Eve imagined someone interested in Carlos might want to intervene... interrupt a rendezvous...

"So now that Crystal is out of the way, who is taking

her place?" David asked again, almost as if he wanted to catch Carlos in a lie.

"I've decided to play it safe and spend some extra time with everyone."

Because one death had been enough?

He finished his drink and surged to his feet. "If you'll excuse me, I have a rehearsal to oversee."

"Don't leave town," Eve said under her breath.

David waited for Carlos to be out of hearing range. "What do you make of all that?"

"He's hiding something, and if he's not, he should have suggested you check the security cameras. Then again, we didn't really think of that straightaway. Still, if he's innocent of any involvement or if he doesn't know anything, then he should have made an effort to clear himself."

"I'm still kicking myself over the security cameras. Can't believe it didn't occur to me." David took a drink of his beer. "Did you get anything else out of that conversation?"

"It's odd. Someone working so closely with that group should really be aware of personal rifts but he didn't mention anyone in particular." Eve frowned and wondered if Carlos had tried to throw them off the scent.

"Would you be happier if he'd tried to find a scapegoat?"

"Of course," she grinned, "That would be a sure sign of guilt." In her books, at least.

"So you think he's covering for himself... or for someone else?"

"That would be my guess. He's covering for someone else." She smiled. "Or himself. Mira will tell you I have a knack for suspecting anyone and everyone." Eve glanced around the bar. "Including the bartender. Did you notice how he didn't move far from us?"

"You're determined to include the crew as suspects."

"If I don't and one of them turns out to be the killer then I'll be the one kicking myself. I've had a few close encounters with mad killers and let me tell you, it's no fun having a gun pointed at you. Luckily, I managed to talk my way out of the sticky situations." Remembering David had worked as a detective, Eve blushed. "I guess you've had your fair share of close calls."

"I have the scar to prove it." David slid off his stool and stretched. "I think we should start taking more care. Remember, the killer's choice of weapon leaves little room for negotiation," he said as they strode out into the open.

"Yes, it would be sink or swim and I'm not a very strong swimmer."

"I wouldn't worry too much about that. The fall alone would kill you."

As they turned a corner, David grabbed her arm and drew her back.

"What? Did you see something?"

"The captain."

"And?"

"He wasn't alone."

Eve edged toward the corner and sprung back. "That's the silver Miranda. She had her hand on his wrist."

"We should casually stroll toward them, nice and easy. Ready?"

As they got closer, Eve strained to hear what they were saying. She thought she heard the captain telling the silver Miranda to relax.

It was enough for her imagination to kick in.

Relax. Don't worry. I've got everything under control...

The moment they saw them, they drew apart. The silver Miranda folded her arms and lifted her chin a notch.

Eve saw David giving the captain a nod.

When they were out of earshot, she stopped him. "Okay. That has to mean something. I doubt that was an invasion of personal space. They were standing close together by consent."

"What are you implying, Eve?"

Could the captain be the other male voice Crystal Reid's neighbors had heard? Could the silver Miranda be the other woman intent on—

She sighed. "The police are going to want to find a solid motive. But first, they'll need a thread to follow.

I'm only saying those two looked very suspicious together. It can't be a coincidence."

"Maybe the captain was touching base with the silver Miranda. She might be one of the group organizers. He might have wanted to know if they were all coping with their loss."

"I'm really scratching the bottom of the barrel trying to see the group in a positive light. Sorry, it's all rather murky."

"You're too strong willed to resent their confidence, Eve."

She gave a fierce shake of her head. "I don't resent their confidence. I simply dislike what they do with it. It's razor sharp and honed with an edge of intimidation. I've never seen anyone act so aggressively, for no good reason."

They took the stairs to the next level and came out onto the lobby deck. Great, more restaurants for passengers to wile away their time.

"While we don't have access to the CCTV footage, we might have something worthwhile to pursue."

"What's that?" David asked.

She raked her fingers through her hair. "I met a woman who complained about the noise coming from Crystal's cabin. She said she heard two male voices."

David cupped her elbow and stopped her. "And you waited until now to tell me?"

"Actually, I spoke with both of Crystal's neighbors. Now I can't remember if they both heard two male voices. Anyway, it doesn't matter. At least one of them did." For once, she had good reason to widen her net of suspicion. What if the captain deleted the footage because he'd appeared in it?

"Jack needs to know about this." While David waited for Jack to pick up, he said, "It would help to know if the captain lives anywhere near Crystal Reid."

Yes. Even if they lived in the same city, that would be a connection they couldn't ignore. As they walked, Eve steered David away from the buffet area only to end up heading toward another one.

"Resistance is futile, Eve. And I wouldn't mind a cup of coffee."

As he spoke with Jack, Eve perused the menu only to realize she hadn't even decided on a design for her menu at the inn. Did she want plain white paper or... She sat back and studied the color. She wouldn't call it beige. Deciding it looked more like sand, she folded it and tucked it into her back pocket for future reference.

"What did he say?" she asked when David got off the phone.

"That we make a great team."

"He is a natural born flatterer... when he wants to be. But how did he say it?"

David looked puzzled.

"If I'm involved in the investigation, Jack tends to employ an underlying hint of sarcasm. Only because he gets tired of warning me to stay away from trouble."

"He did tell me to watch your back."

"And did he sound distracted when he said that?"

"Actually, yeah, he did."

Eve smiled. "That's because he'd switched over to auto pilot."

"Just how many incidents have you been involved in?"

"Let me see... There was the first one when I arrived on the island to visit Mira. Then there was the one when I tried to set up a viewing of an artist's studio for Jill. She's my friend on the island. Jack would tell you she's more than that."

"Co-conspirator?"

"Yeah." She laughed. "Oh, and an old nemesis came to the island to get married. In the end, she didn't."

"Because..."

She bobbed her head from side to side. "She lost her fiancé." Eve took a sip of water and tried to hide her smile. "Oh, I nearly forgot the murder case before that. A friend had put her house on the market and I was looking after it... Well... a body turned up. Then I bought the house, but I fell in love with an expensive stove. So I had to figure out how to find some extra money, and my old school nemesis came up with the idea of hiring out the house to a film company." Eve drummed her fingers on the table.

He lifted an eyebrow. "And?"

Eve hoped it didn't put David off coming to visit the island. "One of the crew met with an unfortunate end."

"And you had nothing to do with any of those murders."

"Of course not, but I was held under suspicion for all of them." She smiled. "All's well that ends well. Jack makes me happy. While he might sound complacent, he really does mean it when he tells me to stay out of trouble."

David's cell beeped.

Reading the message, he gave a small nod. "It's a yes. They're both from Philly. In fact, the entire group is spread around that area. I guess it pays to be overly suspicious."

Eve grinned. "That's two more suspects to our list. Although the silver Miranda was already on it by association. I guess we've got our work cut out for us."

"Jack warned me you'd say that."

Chapter Eight

THE MUSICAL THEATRE DIRECTOR, the cruise ship captain and ninety-nine Carmen Miranda impersonators. There had to be a joke in there somewhere...

Unfortunately, Eve failed to see the humor in it.

Ninety-nine. Far too many suspects to sift through. Somehow, they had to whittle the list down to a manageable number.

Eve had hoped Carlos would mention at least one troublemaker, but he'd remained annoyingly impartial and that left her and David with no leads.

They needed an inside person—someone to provide them with insight into the inner workings of the highly competitive troupe. Eve would settle for overhearing a complaint about someone. That would be enough to give them a few crumbs to follow.

She left David and made her way back to her cabin.

As she approached the elevator, she encountered a group of immaculately dressed passengers. While up on the top deck, the light breeze had played havoc with her hair and the t-shirt she wore had seen better days, but it remained one of her favorites with tiny daisies printed on it. Succumbing to a bout of self-consciousness, she decided to take the stairs.

Along the way, she tried to figure out what she could wear for the rest of the day but then realized there'd be no way around having to change again for dinner. Only two days into her cruise and she couldn't help finding this life of leisure exhausting.

If only that could be her biggest concern.

Reaching the bottom of the stairs, she made sure she was on the right deck and turned a corner. Pay attention, she told herself. Danger could lurk where she least expected it. If this murder had happened on the island, Jack would be advising her to travel in pairs.

She looked up in time to see someone emerging from one of the cabins. A Carmen Miranda. Instinctively, Eve steered herself closer to the opposite wall.

She wore a white wraparound dress with the standard slit down one side but no turban. Her hair hung loose around her shoulders and Eve noticed she held the turban in her hands. The impersonator moved too quickly so Eve didn't see the adornments on it.

As she walked past her, Eve turned and tried to catch any discernible traits in the way she moved. The woman gave her hair a flick and Eve caught sight of her dangly earrings.

Bright purple grapes.

Had she been part of the Carmen Miranda rumble on deck the first day?

Eve didn't notice anyone else around. Feeling slightly vulnerable, she hurried her steps.

Do not, whatever you do, forget there is a killer at large and one Carmen Miranda too close for comfort...

Distracted by her thoughts, she nearly missed her cell phone ringing. She scrambled to retrieve it from her pocket. "Hello," she said without checking the caller ID.

"Have you caught the killer?"

"Jill." Hearing her friend's voice put a light spring to her step. "We should have, but someone is tampering with our investigation. We were relying on surveillance footage from the CCTV cameras but they've been taped over."

Jill chuckled. "And that prompted you to point the finger of suspicion at the captain and his crew."

"You know me too well, but there's reason to suspect him and his crew." At least by her reckoning. "The hairdresser and masseuse clammed up on me. That means someone is pulling the strings. Someone they're afraid of. Someone in a position of authority." Eve frowned. "The captain is somehow involved. Otherwise, why would he interrogate his crew?"

"How did you find all this out?"

"Someone I met overheard the conversation between the servers."

"Two days into your cruise and you already have people doing the legwork for you. You haven't lost your touch."

"Did I mention David Bergstrom?"

"No. Who's he?"

Eve told her about the retired detective. "Jack scoured through the passenger list. Would you believe it... he found two people he knew. The detective and his first grade teacher." And he'd probably searched the list out of sheer desperation since the alternative would have been to suffer through the nightmare of knowing Eve was on the loose by herself. "And guess what? Mira has a thing for David Bergstrom. I've never seen her lost for words. I think she's fallen hard for him."

"And he lives nearby?"

"A few hours away. I wouldn't be surprised if we have a new addition to the island. David might even be one of my first customers at the inn."

"What a fabulous idea. Your own in-house detective."

"Hey, I hadn't thought of that." And she shouldn't take the idea seriously. There couldn't be any more incidents on the island. Surely... not.

"Now I feel I'm missing out on the fun. Do you want to brainstorm?" Jill asked.

If she'd been back on the island, she and Jill would have covered all available surfaces with notes and endless lists of suspects. "Okay, here goes. What would you do in the captain's place?" She reached her cabin and stopped for a moment. "If you wanted to cover your tracks. Would you pretend to question people?"

"Yes. Divert attention away from me," Jill agreed. "That makes sense."

"When I thought the captain wasn't doing anything to investigate the death, I immediately put him under suspicion. I'm sure he picked up on my vibes and decided to throw me off the scent."

"Poor guy. He can't win. But what reason would he have for murder?"

"You want a motive?" Eve scratched her head. "It's bound to come up when he confesses."

Jill laughed. "Thanks, I needed that, but you know the police won't act unless they have good reason to. Come on, you're not even trying. You can do better."

Did she need to remind Jill she was on vacation? "I really don't have much to go on with."

"Come on, you can do it."

"Okay. Crystal's been on this particular cruise ship a few times."

"Did you say Crystal?"

"Yes... she's the victim. Crystal Reid. Jack knew her name all along, but he didn't share the information with me. I found out her name at the hair salon." Eve made a mental note to give Jack a piece of her mind. "Why did you sound surprised when I mentioned her name?"

"I came across the name, but I'll tell you later. Anyhow, you were saying..."

"What if Crystal had something going with the captain? I know it's way out there, but it's possible. Maybe... okay... it's actually highly unlikely. He's not exactly a catch, and she had to have been twenty years younger than him, so I can't really picture him as Crystal's love interest." So much for that theory.

"But if you could," Jill said, "Do you think he might have had reason to kill her?"

"Does a crime of passion need a reason?"

"Yes. Even if it's warped. Every killer we've encountered had a reason."

"Let me think." Eve sighed. "He doesn't wear a wedding ring, but that doesn't necessarily mean he isn't married."

"What if he is married? They've been having an affair and Crystal threatened to tell his wife about them."

Eve smiled. Anyone else would have been quick to dismiss the idea as too unrealistic, but not Jill. "That's a possibility. Let's assume he likes to play around and he always promises he's going to leave his wife, but he never does. Crystal might have decided she'd had enough and threatened to tell everyone about their affair, including his wife. The threat of exposure would have prompted the captain to suddenly remember his loyalty to his wife. They argued and Crystal gave him an ultimatum, pushed him too far." Eve gave a firm nod.

She'd buy that. "What else could Crystal threaten him with?"

"Anything that might jeopardize his job," Jill suggested.

"I like that." Eve let herself into her cabin and collapsed on the sofa. "The hairdresser said something about suspicious activities on board. She didn't go into details but the possibilities are endless. Throw in some sort of financial gain and someone would have a solid reason to kill." Eve sighed and stretched her legs out. "This is exhausting. I'm so glad David is here to handle everything. I've decided I'm going to kick back and relax, even if it kills me."

"I hope it doesn't come to that. I'd miss you."

"So how are things down your end?"

"Deadly quiet. Everyone is asking when you're coming back."

"They're already missing me?" She remained a newcomer to the island and assumed it would take an eternity to be perceived as one of their own.

"Don't sound so surprised. I think the locals have become addicted to your special knack."

"My what?"

Jill murmured something under her breath.

"I didn't catch that."

"You weren't supposed to."

"I can't think of anything that sounds remotely like death knell so I'm sure that's what you said."

"I'd be more concerned about what it says about the

people living here. They can't wait for you to open your inn. Business is going to be booming. You should think about expanding the services to include a café or restaurant."

"I'll already be feeding the guests. Do you want me to widen the net of suspects?"

"You'll have a captive audience. By the way, your new mattresses have arrived. I couldn't help noticing you only ordered enough for ten rooms."

"There are only ten beds."

"Shouldn't you keep a spare? Just in case someone is snuffed out in their bed?"

Two people had already been killed at the inn, or rather, the house she was in the process of turning into an inn. Surely it wouldn't happen again. "While I don't wish to pander to your macabre speculations, I think I should revise my insurance policy. I don't want to be out of pocket every time someone..." she shook her head. There were not going to be any more deaths at her inn. There weren't.

"I can't wait for Halloween. People will be camping outside."

"I'm glad to see I'm still a source of amusement even when I'm not there. I look forward to a welcome home parade..."

"Before I forget," Jill said, "I should tell you why I called. I came across a blog. It's called CM Encore. Yes, in case you're wondering, that's Carmen Miranda Encore. I subscribed to their newsletter and got access to their backlist. It includes photos. I managed to pair up everyone who appeared in that photo you sent me of the fight and put names to faces. I'll send you a list."

"Brownie points to you. Thank you, Jill."

"But wait, there's more. I did a search for the individual names and came up with an article about an incident that happened last year. Drum roll. Crystal Reid took out a restraining order against Bethany Logan. In the photo you sent me Bethany is the one dressed in purple with a yellow turban and bright red cherries."

"How do you know?"

"Because there's a group photo on their blog and it includes their names and she's wearing the same costume."

At last. A suspect with motive.

But she wasn't the one she saw coming out of Crystal's cabin... Eve shuffled through her memory. Had she seen bright red cherries? No, and even if she'd seen cherries, Eve remembered the woman had worn white. Bethany Logan's costume was purple and yellow.

"You're jumping for joy. I can sense it."

"Of course I am. This is the first real lead we have. Someone with motive. Bethany must have been holding a grudge. Did the article give details?"

"Bethany Logan tried to run Crystal over. They'd all been at a function and were leaving the restaurant. Crystal had been about to cross the road when Bethany veered her car toward her. She claimed to have lost control of her car because her hands had been slippery from the hand moisturizer lotion she'd applied before driving off. Anyhow, Crystal reacted in time, moving out of the way but she still suffered a bruise to her leg. Witnesses claimed there'd been an argument beforehand."

"Okay. I'll have to take another look at that photo I sent you," Eve murmured.

"I'll send you a link to the blog so you can compare them."

And then what would she do? Give the information to David. That's what a sensible person would do. She stretched out on the couch and gazed out to sea.

"Have you had any more encounters with the impersonators?" Jill asked.

Eve knew she should have been trying to get close to them, but her instinct kept telling her to give them a wide berth. "Not up close. I've seen them dining and they were all on their best behavior. Now that I think about it, they're never alone." How would she separate Bethany from the group?

She sat up and noticed a piece of paper on the coffee table. Mira had left a note saying she'd gone to the library to make sure everything was set up for the reading.

"I wonder if any of them are readers."

"Why?"

"I need to infiltrate the group and I can only think of doing that if I catch one of the impersonators alone... but in a public place."

"You? Taking precautions?"

"I know. Jack would be proud of me." Eve stretched and yawned. "Trying to relax has exhausted me. I'm so tempted to take a nap but I need to sort out my suspects."

Chapter Nine

"WHAT ON EARTH IS GOING ON?" Mira asked as she came to a stop in the middle of the cabin.

"I'm getting the ball rolling. Hope you don't mind, I borrowed some of your paper." Eve had spent a total of fifteen minutes emptying her mind and trying to relax. She'd gazed out to sea. She'd watched the gentle rise and fall of the waves. She'd even tried to make out an image on a cloud. When she'd pictured a gun-wielding killer, she'd given up. "Careful, you're stepping on one of my suspects."

Mira shifted her foot and stared at the name written in large block letters on one of several pages spread on the floor. "Captain Jon Robertson?"

Eve stabbed an accusatory finger at the page. "Until he can provide adequate proof of his innocence, he will be my prime suspect. His actions have raised too many questions. He's hiding something."

Mira set the book she'd been carrying down on a coffee table and sat down to study Eve's list. "Try to remember he takes his orders from the cruise line owners. His actions might not necessarily reflect his personal beliefs."

"That's no excuse. When it comes to death, loyalty to one's employers must come second. Do you think David would agree to cover up for his superiors?"

"He's retired." Mira folded her arms. "While I've only known him a short time... hypothetically, no. He wouldn't. He'd do anything to get to the truth." Mira lifted her chin. "I'm sure he would."

Hypothetically, Eve thought Mira would stick up for him, no matter what. "Actually, would you cover for him if you suspected he was in the wrong?"

Her aunt dropped her arms. Her shoulders slumped as she pushed out a hard breath. "He'd have to answer some tough questions... Justify his actions. I'd have a difficult time of it, but I can honestly say I wouldn't cover for him. Wrong is wrong."

"Relax. He'd have to survive an earful from me first." Her first marriage had turned her into a suffer-no-fools cynic. Then she'd met Jack... Along the way, she'd misjudged people and she'd nearly been killed for her mistakes. If she'd misjudged David... If he hurt her aunt...

He'd get more than an earful.

"So who else is on the list?" Mira leaned down and inspected the pages. "Bethany? Who's she?"

"She tried to run Crystal over."

"And you know that because... Hang on. Let me guess, you spoke with Jill."

Eve nodded. "She rang earlier with some juicy information she dug up."

"You're collecting quite an entourage." Mira laughed. "Eve Lloyd, the pied piper of murder."

"Funny. She said something along the same lines." Eve tore another page from the pad she'd pilfered from Mira and began another list with a question mark on the top. "How's the setup for your reading session?"

"It's a pleasant room full of books. I think they're there mostly for decoration. There were a couple of people reading which always astonishes me because, from experience, I know most people prefer to loll around the pool, spend time at the casino or watch movies."

"Not everyone is like you or Jill, carrying emergency books in their bags."

"I never noticed Jill doing that."

"She has an eReader and her phone has an app for reading books too. But she prefers to raid your shelves." Growing up, Eve had never been much of a reader. That had changed when she'd moved in with Mira. Books lined every available space in her house on the island and now she even owned the island's only bookstore.

"I'm going to order some room service. Would you like something?" Mira asked.

"Coffee, please. Oh, and something sweet. I need to

feed my creative juices." Eve tapped the pen against her chin. "I want to know if we can gain access to the cameras at the cruise ship terminal. If we can't move forward, we should try to retrace people's steps. There might be something of interest."

"Such as?"

"Bethany might have been trailing behind Crystal while they were coming on board. Keeping her in her sights. I witnessed a couple of aggressive moves from the Carmen Miranda lot on the first day. There might have been more before they boarded."

"I doubt you'll be able to get close-up shots."

Eve threw her hands up in the air. "Well, then I've hit a dead-end." She could see Mira struggling to keep a straight face.

"Is this where you start accusing people to see how they'll react?"

Eve pursed her lips, then seeing the humor in Mira's remark, she smiled. "It might be worth a try."

"Even if you find yourself floating face down in the sea?"

"I can't tell if you're joking or seriously concerned about my wellbeing."

"A little of both," Mira said and turned her attention to placing an order for them.

David arrived shortly after the food was delivered.

"I'm glad I ordered more than either of us could eat," Mira said.

He sat down beside Eve and studied the notes she'd

made. When she told him about wanting to look at the footage from the cruise ship terminal, he drew his cell phone out and called Jack.

"See Mira, he doesn't think it's such a silly idea."

"Sometimes in an investigation," David said as he waited for Jack to pick up, "You need to back up and take stock of the information you have at hand."

Mira smiled at Eve. "Drink your coffee and eat your cake. You might need your strength."

"To stay afloat? I'm bringing out the worst in you." She helped herself to a scone and slathered a generous helping of strawberry jam and rich cream. "Yum. The cream is lemon flavored. I've never thought of doing that."

"He'll get back to us," David said as he put his cell phone away. "But don't hold your breath. They might not be able to allocate the manpower."

"I'm only interested to see if any of the suspects liaised with Crystal while coming on board. Who knows, we might catch the captain having what he thought was a private moment with her. We need to start making solid connections."

"Why the captain?" Mira asked.

"I can't rule him out. Not after he refused to take me seriously and insisted Crystal fell by accident."

"This must be one of your sugar rush storming ideas," Mira said. "And, now that I think about it, not a bad one. I like it. Someone might have been behaving strangely even before they came on board. Yes, it makes sense. Some criminals have been caught after they made the mistake of lingering at a crime scene. Why not before..."

"Firebugs hang around," David offered. "Police are always quick to get their hands on video footage of those crime scenes." He brushed his hand across his chin.

"You look concerned."

"It's my thinking face," he smiled at Mira as she handed him a cup of coffee.

"Think out loud, David. Don't be shy," Eve encouraged.

He rested his chin on his clasped hands. "I'd like to know what happened to the scarf you saw hanging on the railing. There one moment, gone the next."

"I thought we'd assumed it had gone overboard."

"But what if it didn't? I'm willing to bet there'll be traces of blood on it."

"You still think the killer used it to wipe the railing?"

He nodded.

"But what good is finding the scarf?"

"It could prove useful in a trial."

Eve thought about it for a moment. "I saw it when I entered the cabin. It prompted me to look overboard. That's when I saw Crystal's body floating. Then I reported the incident. It probably took the captain fifteen minutes to come to the cabin. The scarf was still there, or at least, I don't remember not seeing it. He locked the cabin and escorted me to his office where he spent too much time telling me off for entering someone else's cabin without permission. He actually referred to it as breaking and entering."

"If he didn't remove it, then someone else might have," David suggested.

"Okay, I didn't really want to say this, but I've been second guessing myself. What if I grabbed it on my way back inside the cabin and put it down somewhere?"

Mira patted her shoulder. "You were in shock, Eve."

"You're too kind, Mira. But you'd think I'd be used to seeing dead bodies by now."

"At least you reacted promptly. Anyone else might have..." Mira shrugged, "I don't know, gone into a catatonic state. Personally, I've never had the misfortune of finding a dead body. I'd like to think I'd know what to do, but I've read so many books and seen too many films where someone always goes into hysterics, so I can't vouch for myself."

Eve laughed. "You're not the type to lose your head, Mira. You'd probably start taking notes for your next book."

"Don't worry about it, Eve." David rolled up his sleeves. "Timeline."

"What about it?"

He gave a small shake of his head. "We need more detailed information. Somehow, we have to establish a timeline and we do that by digging deeper." He surged to his feet. "Carlos said he had a drink at the bar."

"Right after he went to see Crystal." Eve jumped to her feet. "There must be a record of the transaction."

"Yes. Even if he's running a tab. I'll be back." With a wave to Mira, he left.

Eve took a sip of her coffee and noticed Mira staring into space. "What's wrong?"

"Nothing." Mira made a helpless gesture with her hand. "It's... foolish."

"Out with it."

"I hope David doesn't think less of me for not knowing how I'd react in a difficult situation."

"Who are you and what have you done with Mira?" Eve smiled at her aunt.

Mira's grin took ten years off her. "I can't believe I just said that."

"You did, and I'm going to have fun reminding you. David is not the type who'd mind you showing a softer, more sensitive side and if he is... well then, he'd be a fool to hold it against you. If you want my advice, stick to being yourself. He already likes you." She hadn't changed for Jack and he liked her just as she was.

Mira fanned herself and took a few deep breaths. "Okay. I'm fine."

"Are you sure?"

Mira gave a firm nod and poured herself another cup of coffee. "Go on with what you were doing."

"I'm wondering how I can contribute to the timeline. I took my photo at eleven and Crystal was on it." She drew out her cell phone. "Can you access your email, Mira?"

"Yes."

Eve sent her a copy of the photo along with the link Jill had sent her of the CM Encore blog. "If you can open the photo in your laptop, we'll get a better look at it." Moments later, the screen filled with the image and they got to work. If they'd been back on the island and in the comfort of Mira's sitting room, Eve and Jill would have covered all available surfaces with notes and brainstorming ideas. The twin share cabin had a sitting area with a small coffee table and a two-seater couch and Eve had already covered the few feet of floor space with notes. Without a printer, they'd have to make do with looking at the photo on the small screen

Mira pointed to one of the women. "We can't see her face, but the color of her costume matches the photo of Lillian Wordsworth on the blog and I swear, the way she's looking at Crystal makes me shiver."

"I can't get over the fact they're all wearing different costumes. Why does that make me think of clowns?" Eve asked.

They both looked at the picture in silence. Then Mira spoke up. "Possibly because of clown registers and copyright. There are official registries to document a clown's unique makeup. I must have found out during one of my writer's block moments. There is so much information online. Type in a word and the Internet sucks you right in. I bet they've all agreed to never cross the line and wear anything resembling each other's costume."

"You think they have some sort of copycat infringement rule?"

"Writers do it, why not fans of Carmen Miranda?"

"If I ever succumb to an obsession, please promise me you'll make me come to my senses."

"Can I start now?" Mira looked up at the ceiling. "A certain bespoke stove comes to mind. You were quite obsessed with it. You still are."

Ignoring Mira's remark, Eve said, "Lillian's death stare looks familiar."

"It might just be her serious face," Mira suggested.

Eve stared at the photo. After a moment, she clapped her hands and threw in a triumphant whoop. "It's the silver Carmen Miranda. She gave me the death stare."

"She looks quite pleasant in the other photos."

"Hang on." Eve shot to her feet. "She's the one I saw leaving Crystal's cabin." She'd suspected it when she'd seen her making a toast. There had been something about her hand gesture that had looked familiar.

"Are you sure she was coming out of the cabin?"

Eve bit the edge of her lip. "The way she moved suggested it. She appeared to walk diagonally along the hallway as if she'd just emerged from one of the cabins. Also, she was picking up her pace. Again, the way one would do when coming out of a room."

"So what are you going to do now?"

"We'll finish putting names to faces and then..."

Would she risk approaching any of them? "I'll figure it out."

Mira checked her watch. "I wouldn't mind a bite to eat. Coming?"

"In a minute. I should change. I wouldn't want to be seen still wearing my morning shorts."

Chapter Ten

MIRA AND DAVID sat at a table by the window. As Eve approached, he stood up and drew a chair for her.

"David, you're a keeper. If I could bottle you up, I'd make a fortune."

"An opportunist. I like that."

"It runs in the family. Don't be surprised to find yourself in one of Mira's books. She tends to draw her characters from the people she meets, not that she'd ever admit it."

David laughed. "I heard about the mad innkeeper. She tells me you think she used you as inspiration."

"The innkeeper is not mad." Catching the defensive tone in her voice, Eve smiled. "She's undercover..."

The look David exchanged with Mira spoke of easy camaraderie. Eve couldn't help silently cheering for them. "What else has Mira been telling you?"

"She filled in a few gaps and told me you're in the process of setting up an inn on the island."

"Yes, I already have a couple of bookings and my new bespoke stove is about to arrive."

Another chuckle. "I heard about that too. You needed the money to buy it so you rented your house to a killer."

"Not on purpose. And it's no secret. I'm sure I told you about that earlier on." It seemed Mira had been talking a great deal about her. As a way to color in the details of island living and make it interesting? Enticing?

"And," David laughed, "You offered full disclosure and told him about a previous murder that had taken place in the house."

"Yes, well..." That didn't make her mad... Eve fanned herself and glancing at Mira, she gave her a raised eyebrow look to encourage a change of subject.

"David started telling me about his chat with Carlos," Mira said, "But we got side-tracked."

She'd almost forgotten about their meeting with Carlos at the bar and now she wished she hadn't been reminded. If only Carlos had given them something to go on with.

At this rate, she could kiss her vacation goodbye.

"When did people stop talking about the weather?" Eve asked.

"I take it Carlos was uncooperative," Mira offered and laughed as Eve pretended to study the menu.

"Meaning he didn't confess to the crime or point the finger of suspicion at someone else," Eve added. "We're in desperate need of a good old-fashioned rat." Eve set the menu down, only to pick it up again. "Put him under pressure and I think he'll sing like a canary." She frowned and remembered she'd decided to step back and work on relaxing and enjoying her vacation.

Belatedly, she realized this had been her intention all along but it had been derailed when she'd remembered she'd taken the photo of the Carmen Miranda rumble... Clearly she was fighting a losing battle with herself. "There's only lobster on the menu."

"What do you expect? It's the Lobster Lounge."

"It is?" Eve looked around them and noticed all the tables had coral pink covers and the flower arrangements were all orange.

Mira smiled. "You blend in nicely, Eve."

She looked down at herself and only then realized she'd matched her blouse with her turquoise skirt. Lobster orange. "Great. I don't have to worry about dribbling on my blouse." She set her menu down and huffed.

"I nearly forgot to ask," Mira said and turned to David, "How did you go finding out what time Carlos had his drink?"

"The bartender didn't work that shift so he suggested I try again tomorrow."

So much for putting together a timeline, Eve thought

and silently thanked Mira for asking the question. Now they could try to enjoy their vacation.

She tried. She really did...

"In Murder She Wrote," Eve said, "Angela Lansbury always found the murderer using phone records."

Mira took a sip of her drink. "You mean, Jessica Fletcher."

"Same person."

"Not really. One is the actress, and the other is the character she played."

"The devil is in the details, Eve," David offered.

Eve tossed the words around. "Do you think we can gain access to Crystal's cabin again? I feel we missed something."

"I'll see what I can do." David leaned forward and lowered his voice. "What's on your mind?"

"Riffling through her personal effects. You're the official police consultant so there shouldn't be anything wrong with it. Who knows? She might have kept a journal. Also, she must have a cell phone. I've seen plenty of shows where the killer leaves a threatening message."

"Yes, and they usually end up killing again when they try to retrieve the phone."

Eve waved off his concerns. "There'll be two of us searching the room."

"Are you offering to watch my back?" David asked, his eyes twinkling with amusement.

"I wouldn't dismiss Eve," Mira said. "She can be quite handy in difficult situations."

"Thank you, Mira." Eve took a sip of water. Lifting her gaze, she scanned the restaurant. When her gaze landed on the Captain's table, she nearly dropped her glass. "This is a new development." And it reinforced what they'd seen earlier...

Mira and David turned to see what she was talking about.

"That's Lillian Wordsworth," Mira said.

"Flirting with Captain Jon Robertson," Eve piped in. "That has to mean something."

David nudged Mira. "I'm guessing Eve is the type to cut the edges of jigsaw puzzle pieces to make them fit."

Eve didn't see anything strange about two women fighting over one man and one of those women taking steps to clear the way for herself.

"We'll see who has the last laugh." Eve focused on the menu. "After careful consideration, I've decided to have the lobster."

If she never ate lobster again... it would be too soon.

Groaning under her breath, Eve rose from the poolside lounger where she'd collapsed after her waddle around to ease her digestion.

One more turn around the ship and she might feel human again. Smiling, she thought about Bronson. She might end up joining him at the gym. Earlier, she'd seen him from a distance. He'd been dressed in shorts and a t-shirt and most likely on his way to meet his torturer. They'd waved and made a few hand gestures to suggest a meeting later on.

Absently, she gazed at the passengers lounging around. They didn't appear to have a care in the world. Eve couldn't see any reason why she couldn't settle into an easy rhythm. She'd already put enough thought into it to turn her efforts into a working vacation. How hard could it be to forget about everything that kept her busy most days?

Including murder, she thought.

She strode through a food court, averting her gaze from the tantalizing feasts, and instead eyed the lush chairs strategically placed to take in the best views, albeit too close to food. Before she could be tempted into taking another break, she pushed herself to keep walking.

With so many people making the best of the pleasant sunny weather outdoors, she had the corridors to herself. And the shops. She stepped inside one and was immediately accosted by a sales assistant.

"I'm only browsing."

"Are you looking for anything in particular?"

Eve responded to the salesgirl's bubbly tone with a smile. While she'd never been much of a shopper, she wouldn't mind taking advantage of the opportunity. However, giving her stomach a discreet pat, she decided it could wait a couple of days. No point in buying something that would fit today and... sag tomorrow...

"No, nothing in particular." And just as well. She caught sight of a prize tag. Clearly, the boutique catered to people who were either gullible or so affluent they didn't care about cost. "Very pretty," she said as she ran her fingers along the sleeve of a blouse. "Is this the quiet part of the day?"

"It's usually like this during the first couple of days. Passengers are eager to kick back and relax. Once they get bored of that, they hit the shops."

Out of the corner of her eye, Eve thought she saw a pineapple... attached to a head. Instinctively and without much justification, she ducked.

"Are you all right?"

"Knee-jerk reaction." To what? Seeing a Carmen Miranda impersonator? "I thought I saw someone I... well, I didn't want to be seen shopping," she prevaricated.

"My sister does that all the time when we go shopping. She's afraid her husband will catch her in the act." The salesgirl shrugged. "We deal with our issues in our own way. I eat chocolate, she shops."

Eve looked over her shoulder.

"She's just gone up the stairs." The salesgirl gave her a knowing smile.

Eve couldn't hold back her sigh of relief. That pineapple had looked familiar. And dangerous. Her senses must have picked up some sort of danger signal. Maybe it had been the Carmen Miranda who'd shoved her out of the way on the first day...

Eve drew out a pair of shorts and held them up against her. They looked to be about her size, but the way she felt at the moment, she didn't dare try something that didn't come with an elastic band. "Sorry, I had a sort of run in with her."

"If you want to avoid her, she usually comes into the shop early in the morning."

"That's good to know."

"I actually don't blame you. She has an imposing personality. I've noticed myself tensing up a bit when she comes in."

"Did I... Did I look scared?"

"Not really."

She was being kind. "I've been feeling slightly jumpy." Eve tried to distract herself with an eye-catching top but her gaze slid back to the salesgirl. "I heard about what happened... you know, on the first day."

The salesgirl didn't respond immediately. Instead, she turned her attention to tidying a stack of sweaters. After a few seconds, she looked up. "What did you hear?"

"You know. The woman overboard incident."

"Where did you hear that?"

Belatedly, Eve wondered if perhaps she should be more careful about sharing information. "I heard it mentioned at lunch. I caught the tail end of a conversation."

"No one's supposed to talk about it in public."

"Because it would upset the passengers?"

The salesgirl nodded. "Ship's policy."

"Was she a customer here?"

"Oh, yes. She was a big spender."

"Really? How big?"

"Black Amex big."

The invite only credit card? One had to be seriously wealthy to own one of those. For some reason, Eve couldn't connect the idea of being extremely wealthy and belonging to a Carmen Miranda impersonator club.

"Holler if you need anything." The salesgirl moved on.

Eve wondered if that was her way of avoiding being dragged into a conversation she didn't want to have for fear of losing her job.

She spent a few minutes looking at the display cases filled with glitzy items. All the price tags had been discretely tucked face down but she imagined they were well out of her range.

After another stroll around the ship she considered making her way back to the cabin when she heard a familiar tune. Eve turned and followed the beat until she reached a set of double doors.

The Starlight Clubroom.

She eased the door open, enough to peer inside.

"Left. Right, right. Left. One. Two. Three. Four." Carlos clapped his hands. "Again. Chin up, shoulders back and smile. Smile. Left. Right. One. Two. Three."

Lillian Wordsworth, a.k.a. silver Carmen Miranda,

came to an abrupt halt and stomped her foot. "It's not the same. It doesn't feel right. When Crystal did it, the rhythm looked smoother."

"That's because she was lighter on her feet. You, my dear, are stomping around like an elephant," Carlos hollered above the music. "Again, do it again."

Swirling around, Lillian turned her back to Carlos. Her shoulders were lifted nearly to her ears. When she swung back, her eyebrows were drawn down into a scowl.

"This is not the same routine. I told you I wanted—" Lillian lifted her hand to shield her eyes from the spotlight shining on the stage. "Who's there?" She clicked her fingers at Carlos. "There's someone there. This is supposed to be a closed session."

Eve took a retreating step but she'd already been spotted.

"Who are you," Lillian demanded.

"Who? Me?" she asked, her voice all innocence.

"Yes, you. Come forward."

Lillian used such a commanding tone Eve couldn't help taking a step forward.

"Turn around." Lillian stomped her foot. "Don't gape like a fish. Turn around."

Eve did as told.

"She'll do."

"I'll do what?"

"Step in and help us in our hour of need," Carlos explained.

Eve gestured with her hand and pointed at the entrance. "I was only passing through."

"She's the right height. Her cheeks are a bit plump but we can overlook that."

They could?

"Be here tomorrow morning. Now you may leave." Lillian Wordsworth waved her hand and returned to her dance routine.

Eve cleared her throat. "Would you mind explaining—"

"Why is she still here?"

Carlos strode over to her. He tapped his chin. "Do I know you from somewhere?"

He didn't remember her? She'd been sitting at the bar when David had interrogated him...

"I have one of those faces. People often think they've met me or they mistake me for someone else."

He shook his head. "We need someone to step in for... someone. The Carmen Miranda Encore Club needs a photo with all one hundred participants. One is missing but they refuse to dwell on their misfortunes." He gave a helpless shrug. "No one wants to remember they lost a member on their anniversary year."

"You want me to..."

"Pose for a group photograph. There's nothing to it. We'll provide the costume."

She couldn't resist asking, "Costume?"

He gestured toward Lillian who wore her trademark silver ensemble. "It's a Carmen Miranda Extravaganza."

And she'd be required to wear a dead woman's clothes. "I'll be here." Her and her plump cheeks.

"Where have you been?" Mira asked. "We were about to go out searching for you."

Striding into the cabin, her hands in her pockets, her lips puckered up as she whistled softly, Eve noticed the slight tension on Mira's face. It spoke volumes. She hated being responsible for it, but she supposed Mira had reason to worry. They were out at sea in what was generally thought of as a small city. The law of averages alone was enough to tip the scales in favor of something happening. An illness. An accident. An assault. A murder... or two.

"I went poking around the ship. Played around with the idea of putting in some time at the gym. By then, I'd walked off lunch so I stopped for a coffee." She'd deliberately delayed coming back to the cabin thinking Mira would appreciate having some alone time with David. "I see you two have been busy." She'd decided she wouldn't tell them about her run in with Lillian Wordsworth. Not until she had something solid she could share with them.

"We've been crunching numbers," David said, "I'm afraid this is the best I've been able to come up with. I managed to catch up with the bartender."

"That's good news."

"Carlos ordered his drink at eleven forty."

That would have been soon after he said he spoke with Crystal.

Eleven forty.

Eve would have been back in her cabin, talking to Mira...

David tapped the list he'd been working on. "You arrived at the scene at midday and saw Lillian Wordsworth leaving the cabin."

Could she be one hundred percent sure? "Well, I assume she came out of the cabin. It looked as if she was walking diagonally across the hallway, but she might have been struggling to find her sea legs or maybe practicing one of her steps..."

"She's possibly the last person to see Crystal Reid alive." David tapped the space between the names he'd written down. "Let's assume Lillian Wordsworth is innocent." David shrugged. "She might have knocked on the door and when no one answered, she would have gone on her way. We now have to account for this twenty minute gap."

Something they'd be able to do with no problems if they had access to the video footage. "Carlos and Lillian were not the only ones to have contact with Crystal Reid. There were others. Remember I spoke with Joanne who has the cabin next to Crystal's. She said she heard several voices. And so did the woman in the other cabin. Although, I'm not sure how reliable her memory is. She said she'd been partying before coming on board..."

"Did you get her name?" David asked.

"No. It didn't occur to ask."

David sat back. "We need to speak with Lillian Wordsworth. Maybe she saw something... or someone."

Eve couldn't decide if she should tell them she'd been invited... commanded to participate in a photo shoot. Her practical mind insisted it would be a good idea to have some sort of backup. If Mira and David knew what she was getting up to and something happened to her, then they'd raise the alarm. "I think I can do that."

"Isn't she the one who gave you the death stare, Eve?" Mira asked.

"I might have been hasty and judgmental. What I call a death stare appears to be her natural look."

"And you know that because..." Mira prompted her.

"Is that coffee?" Eve asked.

"Yes, would you like some?"

Eve cast her eyes over the coffee table. She didn't want to ask the obvious question. Mira and David had had dinner in the cabin. "It's a bit late for me." Then again, she didn't think she'd get any sleep. She sat down next to David. "I didn't want to say anything... in case I met another dead end." She told them about her walk after lunch and how she'd happened upon a rehearsal session. "The door had been left slightly ajar." Sort of...

Mira looked at David. "Eve tends to read those as open invitations."

"Strangely enough, I was drawn in by the music. It grows on you. Anyway, Lillian was practicing some steps and, from what I saw, she wasn't getting them right. Also, she sounded annoyed because she kept saying the steps didn't look like—"

"Yes?"

Eve closed her eyes and ran through the conversation she'd heard. "She was learning someone else's steps."

Mira put her hand up. "Let me guess, Crystal's routine."

"Yes. Does that strike you as odd?"

"A little," Mira admitted. "Lillian must have her own routine. Why would she want to learn someone else's?"

Eve twirled an imaginary mustache. "Because it's better. Because she's been secretly admiring it. Coveting it to the point of entertaining nefarious intentions."

Both Mira and David stared at her, their eyes unblinking.

"Hey, people have killed for less." She sat back and closed eyes only to spring them open again. "Did I say the door to Crystal's cabin had been left ajar?"

"Yes."

When Eve had gone chasing after the Carmen Miranda impersonator, she'd swear Crystal's door hadn't been open...

"You look pale," David said.

"Do you remember suggesting the killer might have been in the cabin while I was there?"

He nodded.

She closed her eyes again and saw herself rushing toward the elevator and then walking back toward Crystal's cabin. In that time, the killer had tried to make his... her getaway and that's the reason why the cabin door had been left open. He or she had heard Eve coming back...

Chapter Eleven

EVE'S HEART gave a hard thump against her chest. She dragged in a breath but it lodged in the back of her throat.

What had come over her? Eve Lloyd did not cower or shy away from a challenge. Not usually... Hardly ever.

Pressing her hand against the Starlight Clubroom door, she peeked inside.

Cherries. Pineapples. Bananas.

Ninety-nine Carmen Miranda impersonators. All talking at once. A killer hiding in plain sight. Or rather, among a bunch of bananas.

She jumped back. Before the door could close, someone brushed past her and entered.

"Coming in?"

The polite gesture took her by surprise. Then Eve noticed the woman wore a pincushion on her wrist and a tape measure around her neck. She wasn't a Carmen Miranda.

"I'm actually waiting..." To scrape together enough courage, she silently thought. The moment she stepped inside, she would be at their mercy. It would be her against ninety-nine of them.

The woman shrugged and strode inside the clubroom leaving Eve to consider her options.

Accepting the invitation to step in and take the place of a dead woman had left her with no options and, in reality, it hadn't been an invitation but rather a command. And a timely one too since the order had been issued shortly after she'd wondered how she could infiltrate the inner circle.

Jill would insist it had been the result of her asking for something specific and receiving it without much effort on her part. Eve was fast coming round to Jill's way of thinking. When she'd fallen in love with a fancy French stove priced out of her range, the money had come to her from an unexpected source... without any real effort on her part.

Should she perhaps ask the invisible powers that be to point the killer out to her? From a safe distance... and without any risk to her life... or the lives of those dear to her.

Eve nibbled the edge of her lip.

She didn't think she'd left anything out.

Feeling a renewed sense of confidence, she stepped inside the Starlight Clubroom.

Hardly anyone noticed her. After a sweeping glance around, she made a point of committing details to memory. Costumes. Colors. Faces. Mostly, she kept an eye out for anything that might strike her as familiar.

She gave herself a few minutes to adjust to the scene and then she began her search for Lillian... She had to be here. Her and Bethany Logan.

She brought to mind Bethany's costume. Purple with a yellow turban and bright red cherries.

"There she is."

She turned and saw Carlos approaching her, his hands extended in welcome.

"Everyone's excited."

Yes, Eve could feel the energy buzzing.

"Come through to the dressing room. We have someone to help with any adjustments you might need."

Eve hoped her smile hid her feeling of dread. She followed Carlos backstage and into a dressing room. Large mirrors lined one wall reflecting several racks of costumes on the opposite side. The hive of activity mixed with the flow of chatter had her straining to focus. Pay attention, she told herself.

"Everyone," Carlos clapped his hands. "This is our one hundredth Miranda."

The drone of voices faded to whispers and then the room fell silent. All eyes were pinned on her as everyone regarded Eve with curiosity.

Eve watched for anyone showing something other than general interest, but their scrutiny didn't last long.

Within seconds, they all lost interest in her and returned to chatting or adjusting their clothes.

"This is Genie," Carlos said, "She'll help you out with your costume."

Eve turned toward Genie. The woman who'd entered the clubroom ahead of her had a couple of pins protruding from the corner of her mouth. She removed them and, with one sweep of her eyes, she appeared to take Eve's measure.

"You're about the same height as Crystal. I think the clothes will fit you fine." She gestured for Eve to follow her.

"Did you know Crystal?"

Genie nodded. "I met her last year when I first started working here. She kept me busy. Unlike the others, Crystal liked to change her outfit to suit her mood."

"And the others didn't mind?"

Genie leaned in. "They might have, but none of them had the nerve to voice their opinions. Crystal had too much pull."

Before Eve could ask what she meant, someone drew Genie's attention away.

Eve caught a few surreptitious glances thrown her way. So far, she'd spotted one Carmen Miranda she recognized from the first day having her makeup done and another one tending to her headdress fruit salad. However, Bethany and Lillian were nowhere to be seen.

"Here, try this on for size." Genie handed her a white wraparound dress.

One look at it was enough for Eve to know it would be the most revealing dress she'd ever worn. The plunging neckline alone made her want to take a small step back.

"White's not really my color." Eve knew it could have been worse. The day Crystal had gone overboard, she'd been wearing lime green and orange...

"Don't worry. It'll work. I'll make it work."

Eve cringed. "But white is so revealing and... unforgiving. It makes my hips jut out."

"You have a natural curve. Nothing to complain about."

She sucked in her stomach but two days of indulging in anything put in front of her turned her efforts into a losing battle.

"Really, don't worry. The necklaces and headdress will balance it all out."

She'd forgotten about the headdress. Before she could think of dragging her feet with another lame excuse, Eve went to stand behind a partition and made quick work of changing out of her clothes and into the costume.

"I guess it shouldn't be too difficult. I'll only have to stand still for the photo." With any luck, she'd be well out of sight in the back row. Eve stepped out and went to stand in front of the mirror. The shoulder pads had shifted so she looked off kilter.

Smiling, Genie adjusted them for her. "They'll stay in place. You won't have to worry, the routine should be simple enough for you."

"Routine?" She shook her head. "Carlos didn't mention anything about a routine." And if he had, she would have backed out of the deal without a second remorseful thought.

Genie drew her shoulders back. "Straighten your back and lift your chin."

Eve frowned. While she'd never thought she'd had problems with her posture, she looked at her reflection, did as told and saw the difference.

Not sure I like looking down my nose, she thought.

She slanted her gaze toward a woman standing nearby. She had a haughty air about her. Springing her gaze back to the mirror, Eve saw the same haughtiness reflected back.

Lifting her chin a notch, the haughtiness increased.

She lowered her chin.

Raised it.

Lowered it.

Raised it again...

She'd had no idea her chin possessed so much power.

"Okay, now for the makeup." Genie waved to someone across the room. "Martina will take care of you and then I'll come back and we'll work on the rest."

While she waited, Eve checked to see nothing would

spill out if... when she moved. The woman sitting next to her smiled and leaned toward her.

"I haven't seen you around."

"I'm a stand-in for Crystal Reid."

"Oh... I suppose that makes sense."

It did? The woman didn't even bat an eyelash. How could she be so relaxed when one of their own had met with an untimely end?

"We spent months trying to decide how we were going to commemorate the event. Lillian insisted on symmetry."

"Symmetry?"

"For the photo. We didn't want to just huddle together and smile for the birdie. Anyway, we voted on ten different layouts and finally agreed on five rows of twenty. I'm number thirty-seven. What number do you have?"

"I haven't been given one."

"Lillian," the woman hollered, "She doesn't have a number."

Eve shrunk into her chair but as Lillian approached, she sprung back upright and lifted her chin.

Lillian's eyes narrowed.

Eve thought she caught a hint of accusation.

"You came."

Why did she sound surprised? She hadn't been given a choice. Had she?

Eve nodded. "Of course. I didn't want to miss the opportunity. It sounds like fun."

And the Fake Enthusiasm award goes to...

Lillian handed her a square piece of paper. "Pin this to your waist."

Number fifty.

Eve did a quick mental calculation.

Twenty per row. Five rows.

She'd be right smack in the middle.

She imagined Crystal insisting on taking centre stage. But how had she managed to secure the prime position? Just how much power had she held?

"Everyone is expected on the stage in fifteen minutes. They'll call out your number. Don't be late."

Lillian held her gaze for a moment. Eve supposed she wanted a response from her, but all Eve could think about was asking her if she'd killed Crystal.

Sure, I'll be there. By the way, Lillian... did you kill Crystal?

Eve gave a small nod and waited for Lillian to leave. When she did, Eve sank back into her chair. She didn't dare cross the woman. Somehow, she had to figure out how to make a beeline toward the heart of the matter and confront her. After all, Lillian had been earmarked as a person of interest.

A tap on her padded shoulder had her looking up.

"I'm Martina and I'm going to transform you. Tip your chin up and sit still." Martina took a moment to study her face and then set to work.

Eve watched in utter amazement as her face became unrecognizable. Her eyes lost their wide-eyed... surprised expression and took on a vixen slant and, with one masterful stroke of a brush, she acquired high cheekbones.

It took all her willpower to snap out of her stupor and remember she had a mission to accomplish.

"Did you do Crystal Reid's makeup?"

Martina nodded. "You have similar eyes, although you have a slight deer caught in headlights look. Relax."

"I heard there was some bad blood between her and a few people in the group."

"That's nothing new. Get a bunch of women together and there's bound to be a bit of hen pecking."

"Did it ever get out of control?"

"I witnessed a few tantrums."

"Really? Between Crystal and..."

"Everyone."

That didn't help.

"She liked to pull her weight around." Martina shrugged. "Then again, she could afford it."

"Are you saying there was money involved?"

"Of course. She picked up the tab."

"For meals?" Eve asked.

"For everything."

Eve's eyes widened in astonishment. "The cruise?"

Martina gave a distracted nod. "She always made a point of letting everyone know."

Eve made a rough calculation. Crystal's contribution

should have put her on a pedestal. Yet she appeared to have made more enemies than friends.

Moments later, Martina applied a generous dab of fire engine red to her lips. "Perfect. Don't bite your lips."

Eve was about to say she wasn't a lip biter when she had to fight back the urge to nibble the edge of her lip.

Martina leaned down and whispered, "And watch your step."

"What?" Eve asked, her wary expression back in place.

"Competition is stiff. Just watch yourself."

Surely everyone would want everyone else to look their best in a group photo.

The thought faded as Genie returned. She pinned Eve's hair back and placed a plain white turban on her head.

So far, so good. She'd been spared the fruit salad!

Eve's relief didn't last.

"Sit still. I need to secure this in place."

She watched as Genie set a wire frame on her head. Before Eve could ask what purpose it served, Genie settled a pineapple into the cradle. Adding the rest of the fruit took care of hiding the frame.

"Is that a real pineapple?" she asked, her voice loaded with disbelief.

Genie gave a small nod. "Crystal insisted on it."

Eve's head wobbled slightly.

"It'll all stay in place but you have to keep your

back straight. Whatever you do, don't tip your head forward... or backward... or sideways. Just stand still."

Several strands of colorful necklaces and braces later, she heard her number called out. Eve scooped in a breath and followed the procession out to the stage, her attention fixed on not putting a foot wrong because if she did, she'd have ninety-nine Carmen Miranda impersonators to contend with.

A platform of five rows increasing in height had been arranged in the middle of the stage. Carlos stood at the front issuing orders and calling out numbers starting with the back row, from highest to lowest. While Eve focused on making sure nothing fell off her head, she managed to send her gaze skating across the crowd in search of Bethany Logan and anyone showing signs of evil intentions. If the killer stood among them, she wasn't giving anything away.

The line moved. Eve dropped her gaze to make sure she didn't trip over herself, and then took a tentative step forward.

She watched as the rows filled up and she told herself to be patient. Someone was bound to make a mistake, give themselves away... or say something to incriminate—

"How does it feel to step into a dead woman's shoes?"

Eve tensed and wobbled slightly in her high heels.

"No. Don't turn around," the woman whispered.

She couldn't turn around even if she wanted to...

Her pineapple tittered slightly. Eve's hand shot out to steady it.

Could she remember who'd been standing behind her? She'd heard the number called out, but she hadn't matched the number to a face.

Eve drew in a steadying breath. She'd been so fixated on keeping herself together and not putting a foot wrong, she hadn't been paying attention to anything else. Apart from the woman who'd sat next to her in the dressing room, no other Carmen Miranda had engaged her in conversation.

"That's okay. You don't need to answer."

Did she recognize the voice? There were no mirrors out here so she couldn't hope to catch her reflection. The line moved again, but not fast enough for Eve's comfort. She tried to shift slightly in the hope her peripheral vision would catch something...

"I mean it. Don't turn around."

Eve strained to hear what else she'd say.

"You nearly gave me a heart attack. From the back, you look just like her."

Oh, boy!

Okay. Stay calm, Eve.

She didn't want to spook her.

Her.

The killer.

It had to be.

She needed to engage her in conversation. From

experience, she knew killers enjoyed bragging about their exploits. Up to a point.

"Were you friends with Crystal?" Eve asked.

The woman's soft chuckle was drowned out when Carlos called out to the next Carmen Miranda.

"Poor Crystal didn't really have friends here. Then again, she wasn't so poor..."

The line moved again.

"If she didn't have friends here, why did she belong to the club?" Eve asked

"Her mother established the club. Crystal inherited her spot and no one could kick her out."

Not from a lack of trying? Could she ask straight out if someone had taken measures to get rid of Crystal? In the past, she'd used cut to the chase tactics to get suspects so worked up they ended up confessing...

Of course, in the process, Eve had actually put her life at risk. But, she'd known the cavalry had been at hand. Jack had always managed to turn up in time to rescue her. If something happened to her now, David would follow the trail of crumbs... She hoped it wouldn't come to that because as David had pointed out, the killer's choice of weapon left little to no room to negotiate. Once you went overboard, you were on your own...

"I left something for you back in the dressing room."

Eve fought against the urge to swing around. But before she realized what she was doing, she began to turn. As she did, a bunch of grapes came loose and dangled in front of her eyes. Grabbing hold of it, she held onto the rest of her headdress and turned only to find a gap between her and the next Carmen Miranda who was busy with her cell phone. Seconds later, she heard the doors to the clubroom swing shut.

The killer had escaped.

She considered running after her, but just then Carlos called her number.

"Fifty. You're next."

"In a minute," she called out and turned back toward the clubroom doors. Even if she kicked off her high heels and gave chase now, she knew it would be too late.

The woman... the killer, would be long gone.

Carlos called out her number again, his tone impatient.

She'd left...

That meant the killer wasn't part of the Carmen Miranda club.

"Number fifty," Carlos called out again.

Eve made her way to the designated spot and gave herself a few minutes to settle down.

If she hadn't followed the instructions, if she'd turned around... if... if...

Too late now for regrets, she thought.

Moments later, Carmen Miranda fifty-one came to stand beside her. Eve slanted her gaze toward her and nearly fell off the platform.

Bethany Logan stood beside her... wearing purple grape earrings. This was the woman who'd tried to run over Crystal Reid. Eve recognized her from the photo Jill had sent her. And from somewhere else...

Eve mentally clicked her fingers and tried to remember where she'd seen the earrings before. On the photo she'd taken of the fight or on the webpage Jill had found?

No. It had been somewhere else.

She'd never realized thinking required so much moving around and head bobbing. Grabbing hold of her fruit salad, she steadied herself.

Think, Eve.

Where had she seen those purple grape earrings?

Heading toward her cabin!

She silently whooped with joy.

Had it been that morning or the day before?

"You're staring."

Bethany Logan's combative tone put Eve on guard.

She was about to turn away when it all suddenly dawned on her. She hadn't just seen Bethany before.

She'd spoken with her.

Bethany Logan had the cabin next to Crystal Reid's. She'd been the one to complain she hadn't been able to sleep because of the incessant bickering coming from next door...

"I was admiring your make-up. You look well rested. I guess that means your neighbor is no longer keeping you up."

Bethany lifted one eyebrow. "She's been as quiet as a mouse."

Carlos clapped his hands and called for quiet. "And stand still. Whose banana is this?" he asked holding one up.

Eve huffed out a breath. If they didn't hurry up, she'd start to ripen.

It took another half hour for everyone to settle into their assigned places. The photographer took several photos and they were all finally dismissed.

"Remember, full dress rehearsals in two hours."

By the time Eve returned to the dressing room, she thought she might have ground her back teeth to nothing.

She made a beeline for the corner table she'd sat at. A quick scan had her growling in frustration.

Nothing.

Kicking off her heels, she changed into her shorts and t-shirt and gave the dressing room table a more thorough search.

Nothing under the make-up case.

Nothing in the drawers.

The woman must have been having fun at her expense. Maybe someone had noticed Eve asking questions or perhaps someone had overheard a conversation about her, just the way Bronson Charles had said he'd overheard the servers...

There was nothing else she could do.

As a few more people made their way into the dressing room, Eve grabbed a banana and snuck out of the clubroom.

On the way back to the cabin, she called Jack.

"I've been wondering when I'd hear from you," he said.

Eve drank in the sound of his deep voice. "Did you manage to get access to the Cruise Terminal security cameras?"

"Are you eating?" he asked.

"I'm stress eating a banana," she said around a mouthful. "I guess you didn't find anything." Eve knew it had been a long shot...

"Crystal and Bethany arrived at half hour intervals so their paths didn't cross."

"Okay. I have another task for you."

"I didn't realize I was moonlighting."

"You're providing an essential service, Jack. Remember, I'm on a ship with a killer at large. I could be next."

"Not if you follow my advice."

"You haven't actually straight out told me to stay in my cabin."

"And if I did, would you listen to my practical, life-saving advice?"

"What's the point of coming on a cruise if I'm going to lock myself up?"

"Strange, I'm sure I heard you say you had no intention of getting mixed up in any of this."

"Yes, well... best laid plans and all that."

"Perhaps you need some incentive to stick to your guns."

Eve let herself into her cabin and dropped the banana skin on a tray by the door. "You think having a close encounter with the killer will stop me now? Been there, done that." Or rather, she'd been in the thick of it and she'd come through just fine...

"What?" Mira exclaimed.

Eve turned and seeing Mira sitting by her computer, her mouth gaping open, she shrugged. "It was bound to happen. The killer hasn't gone anywhere. At some point, she had to show herself."

"When? How?" Mira asked.

"Hang on. I'll put Jack on speaker. Jack, are you still there, or did I give you a heart attack."

"One of these days, I'm sure you will," Jack said. "Fill in the gaps, Eve, before I decide to commandeer a chopper and have it drop me off on the ship."

Jack to the rescue. Eve smiled... "Well, there I was standing in line for the Carmen Miranda photo shoot, when the person behind me spoke to me."

"I think Jack needs to know what you were doing there," Mira suggested. "By the way, they did a marvelous job with your make-up. I'll take a photo so Jack can see."

Eve raked her fingers through her hair and smiled for the camera. This was the first photo she'd had taken... Everywhere she looked, people were snapping photos or having photos taken. She really needed to get into the spirit of it all. Everyone else was... Even David. Eve remembered him saying he'd spent the first day touring the ship and had photos to prove it.

Jack cleared his throat. "Eve."

"Yes?"

"You were about to tell me about your close encounter with someone who has already killed once."

"Oh, yes. Well, there I was scanning the clubroom for any suspicious behavior when the person behind me spoke up. She said I reminded her of Crystal. Anyhow, she also told me she'd left something for me in the dressing room but I didn't find anything. By the time I turned to see who it was, she was gone."

"So what makes you think she's the killer?" Jack asked.

Eve shrugged. Why else would she approach her? Unless... no, Eve couldn't think of any other reason. Lost in thought, she brushed her hand across her cheek. Her fingers came away with a layer of make-up. Remembering the full dress rehearsal in two hours, she slipped her hand inside her pocket.

Her fingers collided with something...

Frowning, Eve removed a folded piece of paper.

Stay out of this or your aunt will meet with an unfortunate accident.

Eve swung toward Mira.

"What?" Mira asked.

"A threat." Her first impulse to spare Mira any further concern was placated by common sense. Forewarned is forearmed, Eve thought. "I've been warned to stop sticking my nose into the murder or else they... she'll come after you."

Mira surprised her by dismissing the threat. "I wouldn't worry too much about it. We'll be sailing into port tomorrow. I don't know about you, but I'm happy to cut our trip short and fly back home. What can happen between now and then?" Mira took the note from Eve. "We should give this to David. Perhaps the police can learn something from the handwriting."

"Did you get that, Jack? Someone slipped a threatening note in my pocket."

"How?" Jack asked.

Another good question. From the time Eve had left the dressing room to the moment the woman had spoken to her, there can't have been more than a couple of minutes.

She must have had Eve in her sights.

Had she been in the dressing room?

Eve prodded her mind for a crumb of information; something she might have seen but not necessarily paid any attention to. But she came up empty. She guessed there'd been a couple of dozen people changing or having their make-up done.

If it hadn't been one of the impersonators, could it have been one of the other make-up artists?

Jack listened without interrupting. She imagined him sitting back, brushing his fingers along the light bristle on his chin as he catalogued everything she told him.

"Before today, I thought... I assumed there were ninety-nine suspects. Now... I'm not so sure."

"And you didn't recognize the voice?" Jack asked.

"No. I might if I heard it again." The woman hadn't sounded like Genie or Martina, but there had been other make-up artists. "I should have put the place on lockdown."

Jack didn't hide his chuckle.

"Laugh all you like. It was probably the closest I'll ever come to the killer."

"I hope so. You only have the rest of today and one more night before the ship docks. Promise me you'll stay in your cabin."

Eve heard the underlying concern in Jack's tone. She nibbled the tip of her thumb. "The woman who threatened me knew Crystal but she isn't part of the Carmen Miranda Encore group. At least, I don't think so. David will have to get a list of people who were there today." She turned to Mira. "Where is David?"

"He said he was going to hover around the Starlight Clubroom... just in case you needed his help."

"Oh, I didn't see him." She didn't dare hope, but

what if... what if he'd seen the killer come out of the clubroom? "By the way, Jack. Have you checked Crystal Reid's finances?"

"Why do you ask?"

"It'd be interesting to know who benefits from her death. From what I understand, she was a wealthy woman."

Chapter Twelve
———————————

"STOP LOOKING OVER YOUR SHOULDER, Eve. David is fine. He's a big boy and can look after himself." Mira didn't look up from the menu, but Eve would swear she hadn't even blinked. She was pretending she wasn't worried.

"Are you sure he knows which restaurant to come to?" He'd promised to watch her back and had said he would keep an eye out on the clubroom from a safe distance but he should have returned at about the same time Eve had finished with the photo shoot...

Mira looked up. Her shoulders lowered, and her smile lit up her face. "There he is."

Wow, Eve thought. Mira must be head over heels if she'd already honed into David's presence.

David approached their table, his expression giving nothing away.

He wasn't alone.

"Bronson," Eve exclaimed.

David drew out a chair and sat down. "So you do know him."

"I do, but how do you know him?"

"I only just met him. There I was, scouting the Starlight Clubroom when I noticed him watching me."

Bronson grinned. "He nearly broke my arm." He rubbed his hands. "I can't remember the last time I had so much fun."

Eve's eyebrows shot up. "Fun?"

"I spent two hours on an exercise bike this morning. Anything that doesn't involve huffing and puffing... and sweating is fun." He patted his stomach. "Although, all that exertion is starting to pay off."

She had to agree. As impossible as it sounded, Bronson looked trimmer.

"Anyway, there I was trying to steer clear of food when I saw David on his stakeout. I don't know how he did it, but from one moment to the next, he'd ambushed me and had snuck up behind me."

"I thought he might have been the killer," David chuckled.

"Yes... but... David, did you remember to keep an eye out on the clubroom door?" Eve asked.

"Yes." David drew out his cell phone. "And I took photos. Including one of you looking terrified. What was that about?"

"I'd just had a peek inside the clubroom. Ninety-nine Carmen Miranda impersonators in full costume can be intimidating." She leaned forward. "Show me what you have. I need to see who came out while I was still inside."

"All the photos are of people going in," David said.

"Huh?" Impossible. "You must have missed it."

"Sorry," Bronson offered, "My fault. I distracted David."

Eve gave him an exasperated shake of her head and then turned to Bronson. "How exactly did you distract him?"

Bronson looked sheepish.

"Oh, for goodness' sake. Get two men together and—"

"What? I made a passing remark."

"About?"

"A woman strode by and Bronson pointed to her legs." David shrugged. "They were... spectacular. I know, I should have known better..."

"Boys will be boys," Mira said under her breath.

David apologized. "Sorry."

"To his credit," Bronson offered, "He's not easily distracted... not that I did it intentionally."

Eve put her hands up. "Fine. Whatever..."

"So how did you go?" David asked, "Did you learn anything new?"

Eve brushed her hands across her face. "I had a close encounter with the killer, but before I could take a look at her, she left." That would have been his cue to fill in the details. "I don't think she was part of the group."

David frowned. "I got a list of everyone who was at the photo shoot and sent it to Jack. He'll be able to cross-reference the names to see if he can find any significant connection between any of them and Crystal."

Jack was going to be a busy boy. In her opinion, it would be far more valuable to find out who stood to inherit.

The waiter appeared and they all placed their orders.

Eve's mind wouldn't stop tossing around the little information she had.

"I'm going back to rehearse a routine. With any luck, I'll be able to stir the hornet's nest."

"Do you really want to antagonize them, Eve?"

"What else do you suggest I do, Mira?"

"Play it safe. We'll be off the ship tomorrow and the police can take over."

"And what if the killer gets off too?" She eyed the brontosaurus-sized steak placed in front of Bronson.

"I missed breakfast," he said, "And my trainer is putting me on a strict diet, so I have to make the best of this meal."

Eve sipped her tea. "David, who gave you the list of people from the photo shoot?"

"Carlos. He was happy to co-operate."

Eve played with her cutlery, paying particular attention to the design on the handle. "If the woman who approached me wasn't a Carmen Miranda, then she might be a crew member..."

David appeared to be in deep thinking mode. He gave her an apologetic smile. "I can't believe I looked away right when I should have had my eyes glued to the door. Even so, I wonder if I would have noticed anything. They all looked the same."

"Don't worry about it." Eve frowned. They all looked the same... Actually, Eve thought there had been something different about all the impersonators. She clicked her fingers. "White. That's why they all looked the same." Everyone had been wearing white, yet over the last couple of days, she'd seen a kaleidoscope of colors... Hadn't Genie said Crystal had been the only one to wear different outfits?

Eve slumped back and worried her bottom lip. "Wait a minute."

Mira smiled. "Something's clicked into place."

"The photo shoot was run with military precision. Lillian was very particular about us coming out as our numbers were called. The woman standing behind me had to have been number fifty-one."

They all looked at her.

"Bethany Logan was number fifty-one. When I finally turned around, there was a gap between me and the next person. That's when I noticed the doors swinging shut. What if Bethany stepped out and then came back in again?" She closed her eyes and imagined Bethany standing behind her. After Bethany taunted her with an empty threat, she decided to cover her tracks by making a swift but temporary getaway. Long enough for Eve to notice a gap. Long enough for her to suspect someone else.

"Talk to her," David suggested. "See if you recognize her voice."

So much for that theory. Bethany hadn't sounded like the woman who'd issued the threats... "I've already spoken with Bethany. Unlike the woman who spoke to me in a whisper, Bethany sounded aggravated. Angry."

"That might have been her way of disguising her voice," David reasoned.

Eve stared up at the ceiling.

"What are you thinking, Eve?" Mira asked.

Bethany Logan.

The killer.

What if the swinging doors really had been a distraction? Carlos and Lillian had organized everyone. The photo shoot had been perfectly choreographed...

No one else could have stood behind her.

It had to have been Bethany.

Eve sat up. "We need a plan of action." She... they needed to ruffle some feathers and get to the bottom of all this before the ship docked.

"I'd hate to burst your bubble, Eve. You only saw the doors swinging shut," David reasoned. "The woman who stood behind you might have headed in another direction. She could have gone back inside the dressing room..."

Eve gave a determined shake of her head. "When I turned, there was a gap between me and the next Carmen Miranda. Carlos called us out in order of the numbers we'd been given. When I took my place, Bethany came to stand beside me because she was number fifty-one. She has to be the woman who stood behind me." She had to be.

"You should take all that on board, David," Mira said, "Eve is looking mulish."

More than ever before, Eve thought as she gazed out across the restaurant at Bethany.

Why would she want to warn her off?

What would be her motive?

Eve imagined Bethany going to a great deal of trouble to confuse her. There one moment, gone the next...

Eve held firm. Seconds later, her expression began to crumble. "Okay. It's quite possible... maybe... someone else stood behind me. There's only one way to find out." She surged to her feet and made a beeline for Bethany Logan's table.

She sat with several other Carmen Miranda impersonators, none of whom paid Eve any attention.

When she reached her, Eve leaned down and whispered in Bethany's ear. "I know it was you standing behind me earlier today. I found the note you left. Don't think you can intimidate me."

When Bethany looked up, Eve sprung back in time to avoid being assaulted by her elaborate headdress.

"What the hell are you talking about?"

"Very convincing, Bethany. But I'm not buying it. You left a note in my shorts. A threatening note."

Bethany's nostrils flared. Her eyes narrowed to slits. She rose and jabbed a finger at Eve. "If I wanted to threaten you, I wouldn't send you a note."

Eve noticed she'd jabbed her left finger at her. Had the note been written by a left-handed person? She wouldn't consider herself a handwriting expert, but she guessed the words would have been slanted. The writing on the note had been scrawled but she couldn't remember if it had been slanted.

"Would you back up your defense with a sample of your handwriting?"

Bethany watched her without blinking.

Eve expected her to laugh in her face. "Humor me," she suggested. "If you're innocent, then you have nothing to worry about."

"If... If I'm innocent?" Bethany blurted out, her tone outraged. "Who do you think you are?"

"You have quite a temper. There's something else I know about you." Eve gave a pensive nod. "Crystal took out a restraining order against you."

Bethany's expression shifted from battle ready to confused. "How do you know that?"

"I have reliable sources. You can't deny the bad blood between you."

"That was an accident and she overreacted."

"Witnesses said you'd been arguing before."

Bethany's arms shot out. "We always argued. That was her nature."

"And yours too, by the sounds of it. Did you plan on killing Crystal or was it an accident? You said you'd been trying to get some sleep but the arguments from the cabin next door kept you awake. Crystal's cabin. Did you go over to tell Crystal to keep it down?"

"Y-you're rambling."

"Did it all get out of control? She pushed you, you pushed her back, all the way back against the railing. Add some pre-existing bad blood between you, and everything exploded." Eve noticed the others at the table had fallen silent and were listening to the conversation.

"I think you need to see the cruise ship doctor." Bethany folded her arms. "Are you by any chance covering your own tracks? Word is you found the body. How did you know to look overboard?"

Eve had expected to get a rise out of Bethany. Instead, Bethany surprised her by turning the tables on her.

"What's going on here?"

They both broke eye contact and turned.

Lillian Wordsworth was cannoning toward them.

"She's mad," Bethany said.

"She might be that but we need her to make up the one hundred."

Bethany's mouth gaped open. "You're kidding. I don't want her anywhere near me."

"Too bad." With one step, Lillian stood between

them. "Rehearsal is in one hour. If anyone is late, they'll have to answer to me."

"Do you want me to replay it?" David asked.

"I can't believe you recorded that. Promise me you won't send it to Jack. He'll never let me live it down."

David gave a throaty chuckle and waved his cell phone. "I guess this is what one might call leverage. Are you going to behave, Eve?"

She lifted her chin. "As a former police officer, you must have well honed observation skills. What did you make of all that? Did anything give her away?"

"I don't know enough about Bethany Logan's normal behavior to make comparisons."

Eve thought about her first encounter with Bethany. She'd been coy. Why hadn't she owned up to knowing Crystal? Worse. When she'd spoken with her, Bethany had pretended she didn't know anything about Crystal's fate. By then, Crystal had already been dead.

David's cell phone rang. He looked at her.

"It's Jack."

She watched David nodding as he listened to what Jack had to say.

"I promise. Yes. Okay, I'll do my best," he said and disconnected the call.

"What did he have to say?"

"Nothing much."

Mira folded her arms. "I don't buy that and I can assure you, neither does Eve."

"Jack made me promise to withhold this from you until the ship docks..." David brushed his hand across his face. "You'll never guess who stood to gain from Crystal's death."

Eve leaned forward. "Of course not and that's why you're going to tell us."

"Her sister."

"Okay. Does Jack know anything about Crystal's sister?"

David smiled.

"You're drawing this out."

"You'll never guess." David hitched his thumb over his shoulder. "If she had anything to do with Crystal's death then it would be a case of sororicide."

"What?" Eve looked over his shoulder. She smacked her hand against her mouth. "Bethany? Crystal and Bethany? Sisters?"

Eve tipped her head back and soaked in some sun. Closing her eyes, she smiled at the sound of laughter coming from the waterslide. Then she thought about the cream she'd slathered on her scone. Limoncello liqueur. She had to remember that. In a few minutes, she'd have to make an appearance at the Starlight Clubroom for rehearsals. She needed to work on her party face...

Sisters!

Did Bethany Logan use anger as a coping mechanism? She hadn't looked at all upset by her loss. Being an only child, Eve didn't consider herself an expert on the subject, but even if they didn't get along, surely Bethany would have felt something for her sibling.

Eve brushed the dismal thought aside and pressed her cell phone to her ear. Thankfully, Jill's singsong tone made her smile.

"They were sisters," Eve exclaimed.

"Crystal and Bethany? Really?"

Did that let her off the hook? Did it mean Bethany couldn't be the killer because... surely she wouldn't have killed her own sister. Her doubts made her grateful she hadn't known about their connection when she'd confronted Bethany...

"I blew my stack and confronted her."

"That doesn't surprise me. In the past, it's been an effective tool for you."

"I might have to find a new modus operandi... Heavens, just listen to me." She wouldn't need a new tactic because this wouldn't happen again. "Anyhow, she turned the tables on me and I lost my momentum."

"I should have been there."

Yes, if Jill had been there, she would have propped her up.

"So what's the plan now? Point the finger at someone else?"

They both sighed.

"I feel we should be concentrating on the second male visitor."

"Is your finger pointing at anyone in particular?" Jill asked.

"The captain is a safe bet."

"Anyone else?"

"Lillian Wordsworth. There's something going on between them."

"Great. Now all you need to do is find a thread of evidence to prove they both had reason to kill Crystal Reid."

"I stole a menu today. Just saying." Eve listened to the silence. She imagined Jill setting her paintbrush down and then arranging it at an angle only to change her mind and straighten it. She then pictured her sitting back and crossing her legs. Jill rarely crossed her legs. She almost always tucked them under her or spread them out when she slumped on a couch. They often did that when they ran out of ideas and murder suspects.

"I thought you'd already decided on the cuisine for the inn," Jill said in a small voice.

"I didn't steal the contents of a menu but rather the paper. I haven't even chosen what sort of paper I'm going to use for my menus. I should have been thinking about that instead of chasing after would-be killers. At this rate, I might end up handing out photocopied pages."

"Strange you should mention paper. I've been

thinking about it too. Specifically, vellum paper. It's quite thick. I'm thinking of doing some watercolors..."

"Watercolor paper. What color does it come in?"

"White. Off white. Cream."

"Cream. I like that."

A seagull hovered over her. In less than twenty-four hours, the ship would cruise into port. Eve and Mira had already decided they'd had enough and would end their trip early. The thought of walking away and leaving behind a killer had her gritting her back teeth.

"Bethany Logan stands to inherit. Who else would gain from that?" Eve couldn't help asking even as she played around with another idea...

Chapter Thirteen

EVE PICKED UP HER PACE.

"Eve, talk to me."

"I'm thinking and walking." Jill had refused to let Eve hang up... just in case. "If I'm late for rehearsal, Lillian will have my head on a platter."

"Well... multi-task and throw in some words while you walk. I'm getting a little worried here."

"Did I tell you about Crystal's neighbors saying they'd heard a couple of male voices coming from Crystal's cabin?"

"I'm sure you mentioned it."

"We know Carlos visited Crystal but we haven't seen any other man acting suspiciously enough to be added to our list... other than the captain but he's been on the list from the start and mostly because he insisted Crystal's fall had been an accident. Now I'm thinking he really did play a hand in her death."

"Why?"

"A couple of times I saw him with Lillian Wordsworth. They looked quite cozy together. Yet we know Crystal had been having an affair with someone. The way Carlos spoke suggested it had been him, but I'm not so sure."

"You think it was the captain, but didn't you say Crystal was too young to have been involved with him?"

"Each to his... or her own."

"No. We've already played around with the idea of Crystal being involved with the captain and... you said you couldn't really see it."

"Because I kept trying to look at it from a biased frame of mind. I can't help it. I'm not a professional crime fighter. I can't suspend all my beliefs. Play along with me, Jill. If they had been involved, how would the captain gain by her death? He wouldn't. We now know Crystal had been wealthy. We also know she'd paid for everyone's fare."

"She did?"

"That's probably why she wielded so much power." Eve frowned. "Everyone wore white for the photo shoot, but Genie, that's the woman who helped me with the costume, said Crystal had been the only one who'd been free to wear what she wanted."

"Are you suggesting they waited for her to die and then rebelled because she wasn't around to object?"

"As petty as it sounds, yes."

Jill hummed.

Eve giggled. "I'm picturing a thought bubble coming out of your head."

"I'm trying to put the pieces together. I'm sorry to say they are not co-operating. You're suggesting Crystal used her hold over the club to impose her own rules. I get that, but I'm not sure about her insisting only she could wear different outfits. It really is beyond petty."

"Did I mention how unpopular she was? Can you imagine how she must have felt knowing everyone relied on her to pick up the tab? This would have been her way to secure the limelight for herself.'

"I can't imagine ninety-nine of them huddling together and conspiring to kill Crystal so they could have the freedom to choose what to wear."

"Why not? People have been killed for less."

"Do we know if her sister has any money?" Jill asked.

"She does now." What if she hadn't had any money before? What if someone had conspired with Bethany to help her gain access to her inheritance... by killing her sister? "Okay... Let's assume that's the result the killer wanted to achieve." Despite Bethany's aggressiveness, Eve couldn't bring herself to believe Bethany capable of killing her sister. "Where does that theory lead us?" Eve stopped and checked to see she was on the right deck. When she saw a couple of the impersonators walking ahead of her, she followed.

"You think someone associated with Bethany killed Crystal because they knew she would inherit—"

"All right. All Right. You've made your point, Jill. Crazy theory. Okay. Let's keep it simple..." Eve suggested.

"What if Crystal threatened to pull the plug and stop financing the trips? That could definitely lead to an insurrection. If the group knew her sister stood to inherit, and assuming Bethany would be easier to deal with, the group might have decided to keep the cash flowing by getting rid of the threat."

"I like that," Eve said.

"In a minute you're going to realize I've reinstated your ninety-nine suspects."

Eve made a helpless gesture with her hand. "Yes, right when I wanted to whittle it all down to one suspect."

"And if you had to pick one..."

"The captain. But..."

"That's a big but. Should I do a drum roll?"

Eve stopped in her tracks.

"Eve? Speak to me."

Eve was about to ask Jill for another minute so she could get all her ducks in a row, when a thought took hold of her.

An odd... stray thought that had sprung from out of nowhere.

"Do you think my behavior is... sometimes... not

always, mind you, just occasionally... out of character... strange?"

Jill chortled. "You seriously want me to answer that? I've known you for a few months, but can one really ever know a person?"

"Jill, this is no time for philosophical delving. Simple question requires a simple answer."

"I'm tempted to say you've surprised me from the start. However, if I really think about it, everything you do has your name written all over it. So the answer is no. You don't act out of character. Why did you want to know?"

"Someone I met recently did something strange." Why had Bronson tried to distract David?

He'd come across David on his stakeout...

Those had been his exact words... more or less.

How had Bronson Charles known David had been watching her back? Why not just assume David was a passenger hovering around, watching the parade of Carmen Miranda impersonators?

"Eve? Are you still there?"

"I can't get off this ship fast enough. Bronson is..." He was a regular guy, keen to get himself back into shape. No, she was way off track with this one. Besides, what possible motive could he have for killing Crystal?

If there'd been a connection between him and Crystal Reid, Jack would have found it.

"Eve?"

"Don't worry. I went off track."

"Share."

"Okay. Let's say the killer is actually someone we haven't considered. He's not in any way involved with the victim. What would be his motive?"

"She saw something."

"Huh?"

"She witnessed something she wasn't meant to see. It's in a book I read recently. A little boy sees something he wasn't supposed to, and is pushed off a window."

Eve drew in a sharp breath. "I asked David Bergstrom where he'd been between eleven and twelve that first day and he told me he'd been on a tour of the ship and there were photos to prove it. Everyone was excited, taking photos and filming."

"I'm not sure I follow."

"We need to think outside the box."

"Because Bronson Charles did something unexpected?" Jill asked.

"It's what gives the game away. Isn't it?" She thought back to their first encounter. He'd been the one to tell her about the captain interrogating his staff. Eve had made the rounds of several restaurants and hadn't heard a single peep, while Bronson had had the good fortune to be in the right place at the right time... What if he'd made it up? Why? For a wild moment, she imagined him as a hired killer. Eve laughed under her breath. Way to go, Eve, suspect all ninety-nine Carmen Miranda impersonators of hiring a killer.

A hard hand wrapped around her elbow.

"I'd like a word with you." The command was muttered through gritted teeth.

Eve recognized the voice. Her heart jumped to her throat. She tried to talk, to say something. She urged her throat to clear.

"Put the phone down."

Eve complied but only because he'd put enough pressure on her arm to make it drop.

"Now keep walking."

Did he have a weapon?

Her reasoning mind told her he did.

She could hear Jill calling out to her. Eve hoped... she prayed Jill would realize something was wrong.

She slanted her gaze toward him...

He looked grim.

Determined.

Eve had been making her way to the clubroom across the other side of the ship. They were halfway there. She could see the atrium coming up. Did she dare scream for help?

Would anyone hear her?

Most passengers were out and about, enjoying the lovely weather. She hadn't ventured into the casino, but she knew it was a popular spot too. There was one located right after the atrium.

If she could somehow create a distraction...

"You'll never get away with this. There are cameras everywhere. Someone's probably watching us right now."

"And your point is?" he asked.

"What are you going to do? Throw all the passengers overboard?"

"What are you talking about?" he asked.

"It really is too late. You're on the suspect list. In fact, I've just been talking about you with my colleague."

He gave her a dismissive grunt. "An amateur sleuth on the ship. I didn't see that one coming."

"Amateur? Well, let me tell you, I have enough experience to know you'll be in handcuffs soon."

"A crazy amateur to boot. You overestimate people's ability to notice or even care. Everyone here wants to have a good time. That's all they think about. They're not likely to notice you or me walking behind you. And that's how I want to keep it."

Eve made a frantic search for something, anything she could use to her advantage. The stairs were coming up.

If she tried to use one of the manoeuvers Jack had taught her, she might manage to throw him off balance and send him toppling down the stairs. At which point, he would have hopefully released his hold of her arm.

"Where are you taking me?" she demanded.

"Somewhere private where no one will hear us. As I said, we need to talk."

If he thought she would play along and allow herself to be walked up the gangplank, he had another think coming. "I should warn you. There's no way you'll ever get away with this. I'm expected and if I don't turn up on time, people will notice and they'll go looking for me."

"Our talk will be over before anyone's had a chance to notice you missing."

Where was a Carmen Miranda impersonator when you needed one?

Before they reached the top of the stairs, he pulled her away and along another corridor.

So much for her plan to push him down the stairs...

She still held the cell phone clutched in her hand. Hopefully, she hadn't pressed anything to disconnect the call. By now, Jill would have alerted Jack who would have contacted David.

The cavalry would be on its way. She had to believe it.

"This way." He opened a door and guided her inside.

The alarm had been raised, Eve told herself even as she searched the cabin for something, anything she might use as a weapon. Why had she let him draw her into this cabin? When had she become a willing victim? No one else had been threatened. There hadn't been anyone else at risk of collateral damage. She should have stood up to him. She should have... What? Elbowed him? Panic set in like cement pouring through her veins. The moment he'd grabbed her, she should have screamed. She should have...

Eve frowned.

Idiot. She held a weapon in her hand.

If she didn't use it now, she'd live to regret it... Even if only for a few seconds or however long it took to hit the water... If he planned on killing her the same way he'd killed Crystal... Eve wrenched her eyes away from the balcony.

She clutched the phone against her.

The moment she swirled around, she could...

Throw it at him?

What if she missed?

No second thoughts, Eve.

Do it now, she told herself.

If she missed her chance, she might not get another one.

Just as she turned to face him, he shut the door.

Eve drew her arm back. In that split second, she caught sight of the kettle. She put all her focus on throwing the phone at him. As it left her hand, she reached for the kettle and swung back just as her phone hit him on the side of the head.

"What the hell are you doing?" he hollered.

"Trying to stay alive," she screamed at the top of her voice, a tactic that had served her well in the past.

The phone must have hit him hard. He'd crouched down enough for Eve to now aim the kettle straight at his head.

With a mighty roar, she put all her weight into it and hit her target.

He went down for the count.

Eve stepped back and stared in astonishment.

She'd done it...

"Too easy."

Grabbing the kettle, she used the cord to tie his hands. Thinking that wouldn't be enough to immobilize him, she grabbed a table lamp and used that cord to tie his feet.

Eve picked up her cell phone. Thankfully, it still worked. She called Jill to let her know she was okay. Then she called David.

"Eve! Where are you? Jack called to say you were in trouble."

"I'm in a cabin off the main atrium. I've tied him up, David. I've got him."

She disconnected the call and waited for the cavalry to arrive. Better late than never...

She looked down at her prisoner.

When his eyelids fluttered open, he gritted his teeth and growled at her.

"Now. Now. No biting," she warned.

"You stupid woman. Cut me loose."

Eve laughed. "Really. That's the best you have?"

"You've got the wrong man."

"And that, my friend, is a cliché. You'll have to do better."

She watched him struggling. "I had my suspicions about you—"

"If you don't cut me loose..."

"You'll what? Throw me overboard?"

He spat out a curse. "Someone else has gone overboard. One of the cameras malfunctioned and didn't tape over itself."

Eve rolled her eyes. "Yeah, a likely story."

"It happened on the first day."

"And what does that have to do with you killing Crystal?"

"I did not kill her."

"So you want me to cut you loose. And then what? You tell me what a stupid woman I really am and push me overboard?" Eve laughed and looked at the screen on her cell phone to see who was calling her.

Jack.

"Tell me you're all right," he demanded.

Eve savored the sound of his voice. "I am now." Jill had contacted him, just as Eve had hoped she would. "It's all over, Jack. Don't ask me how, but I've tied him up. And, surprise, surprise... not, he pleads innocence." And, annoyingly, she wanted to hear the rest of his story.

Someone else had gone overboard? Did that mean someone else had been killed? Before or after Crystal? She and Jill had been playing around with a new theory. What if Crystal had seen something she wasn't meant to?

"We've found something, Eve," Jack said.

Eve sank into a chair.

"We searched Crystal's house and looked through her computer. It took the tech guys some doing but they managed to get in. She took photos of the first day and emailed them to herself. At first we didn't see anything of value, but we had a closer look... Something didn't look right. I cross-referenced the information we have at hand. The passenger names, photos and cabin numbers."

"Jack, I need you to give me the short version."

"There's a photo of a man coming out of a cabin. When we identified him using the passenger list photos, we checked his cabin number. The cabin he was photographed coming out of wasn't his."

Eve tried to make sense of everything Jack told her. "Why would Crystal have taken a photo of a man exiting his cabin?"

"She didn't. She took a photo of one of the impersonators who was standing in the corridor. The man is standing in the distance."

Frowning, Eve looked up and saw the cabin door pushed open. David appeared with Bronson hard on his heels.

David looked grim.

Eve held a finger up calling for a moment. She watched David and Bronson taking in the scene.

Eve looked down at the captain.

He'd tried to convince her someone else had gone overboard...

Turning her attention back to Jack, she said, "At some point you're going to tell me who..." Although, she only needed Jack to confirm her suspicions.

Eve listened to Jack while she watched David helping the captain to his feet.

"Say again."

Jack repeated the name. Eve nodded. It was the same name that had been bouncing around her head, but she still struggled to believe it.

"There is one thing I wanted to ask, Jack." She drew in a breath and called for calm.

"What's that?"

"Are you by any chance planning on meeting me in Florida?"

"As soon as I hang up, I'll be on my way."

"That's a relief. I can't wait to see you again." She disconnected the call and looked up. The captain was spluttering away.

"Yes, yes. That's enough of that," Eve said. "David. Thank you for coming to my rescue." She had to think fast and act even faster. "I don't suppose you carry handcuffs on you?"

David grinned. "As a matter of fact, I commandeered a pair from one of the security guards."

"You are so resourceful."

He gave the kettle cord a tug. "You did a terrific job with this. What do you need handcuffs for? He's not going anywhere."

"Better safe than sorry," Eve said, "May I do the honors?"

"Of course. You deserve all the credit. While you do that, you might want to tell me how you managed this."

"The captain ambushed me along the way. I threw my phone at him and then grabbed the kettle."

"That's thinking on your feet." David retrieved the handcuffs from his back pocket and handed them to her.

Eve knew she only had a small window of opportunity and she didn't want to take any chances. "I don't know what else I could have used to knock him out." Using laughter as a distraction, she made quick work of slipping the handcuff on Bronson.

He instantly snatched his hand away. "What the... hey. What are you doing?" His reaction made her lose her footing.

He pulled his hand again. Eve tried to grab hold of his other hand. When she failed and saw that Bronson intended pulling again, she clamped the handcuff on her own wrist.

"Bronson Charles. I'm making a citizen's arrest."

"What? You're mad."

Eve rolled her eyes. "Why does everyone assume that about me?"

Chapter Fourteen
―――――――――

"GET IT OFF ME."

Bronson yanked his arm back so hard Eve slammed against him.

"Eve." David looked confused.

"It's what I've been trying to tell you," the captain said, "You've got the wrong man. Untie me."

David looked from Bronson to the captain.

Pressing her hand against Bronson's chest, Eve pushed herself off him, not that she got very far. "David. Do as the captain says."

"Are you sure?"

She gestured wildly to the handcuff around her wrist. "You think I did this for fun. Bronson's our killer."

Her timing could not have been worse. In hindsight, she knew she should have waited for David to free the captain, making it three against one. But she'd had to do something. What if Bronson took someone else hostage?

"David, please hurry."

Bronson clamped his free hand around Eve's neck and pulled her back against him.

David now made quick work of releasing the captain. "Don't be a fool, Bronson. Let her go."

"That's not going to happen. At least not until I get a firm assurance you'll provide me with free passage off this ship."

When in doubt... or peril, Eve thought, laugh in the face of adversity. "Yeah, that's definitely not going to happen."

"We'll see who has the last laugh."

Eve gave a brisk shake of her head. "You really had me fooled, Bronson. I thought you were one of the nice guys."

"I am nice."

"When you're not pushing people off balconies. Who else did you kill, Bronson?"

"There's no proof."

The captain rubbed his wrists. "We've got you on camera. A body went overboard and you looked over the balcony."

And then there was the proof Jack had found. "You saw Crystal take a photo of you as you were coming out of the cabin. Someone else's cabin. This other person who went overboard. What did you do then, Bronson?"

She slanted her head to face him. "Did you think the photo would tie you to the crime?"

His nostrils flared. The laughter she'd seen in his eyes before disappeared. "I had to get that photo back."

"So you went to her cabin. Did you ask nicely?" Eve asked in a singsong voice.

"It was bad enough I had to wait for my chance. She had a string of people coming and going. When I told her to hand over the phone, she took another photo of me and she kept taking them. I had no choice."

Eve imagined Crystal telling him to take a hike and when he refused, she took a photo of him and threatened to send it to the police. He'd pushed his way inside her cabin and had tried to snatch the phone off her. That must have been when her fruit salad turban came off.

Crystal had already emailed the photos she'd taken earlier to herself, the ones where Bronson had appeared in the background by accident. Jack had told her the email had a date and time stamp on it. It put Carlos in the clear as well as the silver Miranda Eve had seen when she'd tried to retrieve her luggage. Of course, by then Crystal had been in the water...

Crystal Reid must have been killed five minutes before midday so when Eve entered the cabin, she'd only been in the water for five minutes, still floating. Any longer and she might have sunk or drifted too far away for anyone to see.

"Did you have to push her off?"

Bronson gave her a raised eyebrow look.

She shook her head. "Why does everyone rush toward easy solutions?"

"I gave her the chance. I only wanted her phone. If she'd given me the phone..."

"What?" When Bronson didn't reply, Eve sighed. "Bronson, you didn't plan any of this. I can't have been that wrong about you. Things happen, we understand. A situation can get out of control and before you know it, you're doing something impulsive and you think there's no going back."

He laughed, but not from amusement. His laughter had an underlying hint of evil.

"You think I didn't plan it. I guess that bodes well for me. If I gave myself up and went to trial, I'd only need twelve gullible fools like you to sit in the jury and I'd walk away free."

Although reluctant to admit to being a gullible fool, Eve decided to agree with him. "Yes, and if that doesn't work, you could plead temporary insanity. That should reduce your sentence."

He appeared to think about it.

"No, I'd rather not risk it. Even though I'm in the right. He had it coming."

He?

Eve slid her gaze toward the captain.

"Steve Matherson."

"Who... what was he to you, Bronson?"

"He's the guy who ran me off the road. He put me in hospital for months while he walked away free. He got all his fancy lawyers to get him off the hook. He even managed to convince everyone it hadn't been him behind the wheel."

He'd come on the cruise to kill the man who'd run him over. The perfect crime, he'd thought having read an article about a man going overboard...

"There you go. You were driven by rage. He was guilty and he ruined your life. Anyone would sympathize with that. Don't make this worse than it already is, Bronson."

"It's too late. I'm not paying for this crime. It was his fault."

Eve silently rolled her eyes and wondered why people couldn't accept responsibility for their own actions. They always had to blame someone else...

"Think about it, Bronson. Where will you go? You can't run from this. The police have evidence linking you. Crystal sent the photos to her email account."

"You're lying."

"She probably wanted to clear her phone because she knew she'd be taking lots of photos. And I'm not lying. I was just on the phone with Detective Jack Bradford. That's how I knew you were responsible. The police have joined the dots and Detective Jack Bradford is not going to wait for the ship to dock. A S.W.A.T. team is on its way."

"We're not far off the coast now," the captain piped in. "They'll be here sooner than you think."

Bronson growled. "There are boats on this ship. I

saw one being unloaded when you tried to retrieve the body." His gaze shot around the room. "You. The both of you." He gestured toward David and the captain. "In the bathroom. Now."

"The lock is on the inside," Eve reasoned, "What good will that do?"

"Shut up."

He sounded agitated. Eve didn't want him to do anything out of desperation so she bit the edge of her lip. Whatever came out of her mouth next had to be enough to take his mind off locking David and the captain in the bathroom, but not get him angry.

"You have a whole ship at your disposal. Why settle for a small boat. You'll have greater bargaining power. More leverage."

"What are you saying?"

"You should take over the ship. Then the authorities will have no option but to listen to your demands. They might sacrifice one or two people but if you take the entire ship hostage—"

"The entire ship?" Bronson smirked. "When I first met you, you didn't sound so crazy."

"I am not crazy and neither is the innkeeper."

"What innkeeper?" Bronson asked.

Eve scooped in a breath and shrilled, "The one standing behind you right now."

He looked. He actually looked over his shoulder.

At the same time, Eve went limp. The moment she sensed him loosening his hold around her neck, she put one of her moves into action and aimed where it would hurt the most.

Bronson toppled over. Unfortunately, she happened to be in the way so he fell over her.

He was a tall man with a bulky build. Add to that the excess weight he had gained during his time in hospital... Eve estimated she had over two hundred pounds squashing her.

The more he squirmed in agony, the heavier he became.

She could barely draw enough breath to speak. "Argh! David. Get him off me."

The captain had grabbed a small hand towel and was now using it as a fan. "She's coming round."

Eve groaned. She felt sore all over. Trying to lift her hand, she gave up and let it flop down again.

"Is it over?" she managed to ask.

"Yes. Bronson has been handcuffed properly and is now in the custody of my crew," the captain said.

"Here, I'll help you up," David offered.

"Hang on. Give me a minute. This is the first real moment of relaxation I've enjoyed since coming on board."

She saw the captain frown.

"No reflection on your wonderful ship. Circumstances being what they were, I didn't have a chance in hell of relaxing." She eased herself into a sitting position and wondered why she always ended up flat on her back. At least this time she hadn't had a gun pointed at her.

"How are you feeling?" David asked.

Now that she thought about it, she felt slightly foolish and... gullible. If Bronson hadn't tried to distract David, Eve would never have suspected him. "Where's Mira?"

"Right here."

Mira waved at her from a chair. Eve felt dreadful. She must have been so worried...

"Sorry, Mira."

"What for? Life is never dull with you around, Eve."

"If given the choice, I'm sure you'd opt for a different type of entertainment."

"Not necessarily. Your spills and thrills are quite unpredictable. I never know what you'll do next."

"This will surprise you."

Mira shifted to the edge of her chair.

"How do you feel about staying on and seeing the cruise to the end?"

"Are you sure?"

"Well, you still have your book reading to do. The killer has been caught. There's no reason for us to worry."

The captain cleared his throat.

"I suppose you want me to apologize to you." Eve stretched her hand and David helped her up.

"It wouldn't hurt but it's not really necessary," the captain said.

"Well, what was I supposed to think when you grabbed hold of my arm?"

"That I wanted to have a word with you in private? It's what I said to you."

He needed to work on his communication skills. "Yes, but... if you'd ran into as many killers as I have, you would have been highly suspicious too."

"You really thought I was the killer?" The captain gave a brisk shake of his head.

"We're even. You dismissed my suspicions as the ramblings of a mad woman."

He cleared his throat and straightened. "I'd been prepared to apologize and acknowledge you'd been right, but I wanted to do it in private. We can't afford to have anyone on board upset. It would only take one person to overhear a snippet for rumor to spread on the ship and create panic."

"You might have mentioned that."

"Eve."

She turned to face her aunt.

"Not everyone finds the right words to say. Some people's personalities are so immersed in their professional roles, they forget how to communicate with the average person... that's not to say you're average."

In other words, her aunt wanted her to go easy on the captain.

Eve gave the captain a raised eyebrow look. "I think

what my aunt is trying to say is that next time you should consider choosing your words carefully before approaching a suspicious person such as myself. I could easily misconstrue your actions."

The captain looked slightly confused. "I suppose I owe you an apology."

Eve smiled. Her "Thank you" was drowned out by the sound of the ship's horn.

Epilogue

"WASN'T it nice of the captain to organize the accommodation for you? I'm so happy you decided to take him up on the offer."

Jack put his arm around Eve. "I'm overdue a vacation."

"We'll have to outfit you with some proper sailing clothes. There are plenty of shops here."

"This is the life." Jill tucked her sunglasses in place and stretched out on her deck chair. A waiter stood nearby holding a tray of colourful drinks. "Thank you. I'll have the pretty one with the pink umbrella."

Eve looked at Jack. "Tell me again how Jill happened to hitch a ride with you."

Jack gave a small shake of his head. "I'll tell you just as soon as I figure it out myself. One moment I was on the phone telling you about the photos we'd found on Crystal Reid's home computer and the next Jill was running around the precinct calling out my name. I guess it was easier to bring her along."

"Oh, yes. The road of least resistance."

"I think she's been hanging around you too long." Jack accepted a couple of glasses and handed one to Eve.

"So what's going to happen with Bronson Charles?"

"That's up to the authorities now. They have enough evidence to link him to the two crimes. Considering his history, a good lawyer will most likely try to get him a plea bargain. It's all in the hands of the legal system now."

One that had already failed him once...

"I can't help feeling sorry for him. Honestly, he was a nice guy."

"Who happened to come on board the ship with a ready made plan to kill the man he thought had ruined his life. That's called a premeditated act." Jack guided them toward a couple of deck chairs. "So how many people did you end up suspecting this time?"

"I went from one to ninety-nine and then back to one again. Well, strictly speaking, when I suspected the captain I thought he might have been in cahoots with Lillian Wordsworth. I guess I'm going to have to revise my tactics. It's all well and good to be suspicious, but it can be distracting. For instance, all along I thought I saw the silver Miranda coming out of Crystal Reid's cabin but she'd only stopped by to give her a message and when Crystal didn't answer the door, she left. The arguments the neighbor had heard had been between Crystal and her sister..." Half-sisters, Eve had been told, and they'd never been on good terms. Eve sighed. None of it mattered now. She was on a cruise with Jack. She had to make the most of this. Once she returned to the island, it would be all hands on deck.

When Jack didn't comment, she glanced at him.

He was staring at her.

"What?"

"Change your tactics?"

"Oh... Yes, just in case. You know me. I don't go out of my way to look for trouble." She sipped her drink.

"Not that it matters now that the killer's been caught, but..."

Eve turned to Jack. "What?"

"Did you ever find out who put the threatening note in your pocket?"

"That had me gritting my back teeth. I remembered the note as I watched the senior officers taking Bronson away. I almost stopped them so I could wring the information out of Bronson, but then Bethany Logan appeared at the door." Eve shut her eyes and smiled.

Crystal's sister... or rather, half-sister had finally let her guard down.

Bethany had looked contrite and, despite her snippy temperament, she'd been in tears.

"I'd been right to suspect Bethany Logan. She wanted to scare me off. If her sister's death came under suspicion, it would have delayed her getting her inheritance. Money had always been a point of contention with them. As the elder of the two, Crystal had always held the purse strings and Bethany was in deep debt. After issuing her warning, Bethany stepped out of the clubroom only to realize she couldn't leave because Carlos would have noticed."

When Bethany's guard had dropped, Eve had taken the opportunity to ask if Crystal had been having a fling with Carlos... That too had been clarified. Yes, Crystal had strung Carlos along, but she'd had her eye on a new officer.

Eve twirled her straw around the glass. She was glad her and Mira had decided to stay on and continue with their cruise. She could relax... especially now that Jack was with her. However...

"So... you have another murder under your belt."

"You're mocking me, Jack." She laughed and tried not to think about her close encounter with a killer. "David was marvelous. He's the one who suspected the killer might have kept the scarf." But he hadn't. Bronson had disposed of it as soon as he'd returned to his cabin. He had been in the cabin when Eve had gone in to exchange the suitcases. Just before she'd entered, he'd tried to make his getaway, but he'd heard her returning, so he'd ducked back inside the cabin, leaving the door slightly ajar. Moments before, he'd pushed Crystal off the balcony... after he'd bashed her head against the railing. David had also been right in thinking he'd used the scarf to wipe the railing clean.

Eve took a sip of her drink. "Never mind all that. We're on vacation. It's all over. Time to relax now." She closed her eyes and smiled in contentment.

"Eve?"

"Yes?"

"There's a woman staring at you. I think she's trying to get your attention."

"Oh... I nearly forgot." Eve jumped to her feet. "I have a rehearsal to go to."

"Rehearsal?"

"I've become an honorary Carmen Miranda. The show must go on."

Printed in Great Britain
by Amazon